The Deathbed Sutra of the Buddha

or

Siddhartha's Regrets

The Deathbed Sutra
of the Buddha

or

Siddhartha's Regrets

George Adams

BOOKS

Winchester, UK
Washington, USA

First published by O-Books, 2014
O-Books is an imprint of John Hunt Publishing Ltd., Laurel House, Station Approach,
Alresford, Hants, SO24 9JH, UK
office1@jhpbooks.net
www.johnhuntpublishing.com

For distributor details and how to order please visit the 'Ordering' section on our website.

ISBN: 978 1 78279 612 1

A CIP catalogue record for this book is available from the British Library.

Design: Lee Nash

Printed in the USA by Edwards Brothers Malloy

We operate a distinctive and ethical publishing philosophy in all areas of our business, from our global network of authors to production and worldwide distribution.

CONTENTS

Facts

1. The venerable Ananda was born on the same day as Siddhartha Gautama, later known as the Buddha.
2. Ananda was a cousin of the Buddha, born into the same Shakya clan as Siddhartha.
3. As cousins, Ananda and Siddhartha grew up together in the city of Kapilavastu.
4. At age 37, Ananda left home to become a follower of the Buddha, joining the community of Buddhist monks known as the *Sangha*.
5. At age 55, Ananda received the great honor of being chosen by the Buddha to be his personal attendant (or *upatthaka*).
6. As personal attendant, Ananda was the constant companion of the Buddha for the next 25 years, seeing to his every need, hearing every word taught by the Blessed One.
7. The Buddha's trust and confidence in his cousin Ananda was so great that, at times when the Buddha was ill or weary, he permitted Ananda to teach in his place, an honor accorded to very few of his followers.
8. Ananda became known as the 'Guardian of the Dharma,' for his ability to memorize every teaching, syllable by syllable, ever uttered by the Buddha. At the Council of Rajagriha, convened shortly after the death of the Buddha to establish a definitive canon, Ananda recited over 80,000 teachings of the Buddha, which came to form the bulk of the earliest Buddhist canon, commonly referred to as the Pali canon.
9. Ananda was with the Buddha at the time of the Blessed One's death.
10. Clearly, no one was closer to the Buddha than Ananda; no one had more intimate access to the words of the Buddha than Ananda.

Translations

All verses from Pali texts are from the Wisdom Publications translations, published in *The Teachings of the Buddha* series, specifically:

The Long Discourses of the Buddha: A Translation of the Digha Nikaya, translated by Maurice Walshe (Boston: Wisdom Publications, 1995)

The Middle Length Discourses of the Buddha: A Translation of the Majjhima Nikaya, translated by Bhikku Nanamoli and Bhikku Bodhi (Boston: Wisdom Publications, 2001)

Preface

Many who read the ancient Buddhist document translated in chapters three through eight of this book will undoubtedly, and for good reason, question the document's authenticity. Indeed, I myself, despite having played a direct role in its being brought into the public light, sometimes look back in virtual disbelief: disbelief at how I received it, disbelief in its content, and disbelief that it could have remained hidden for so many centuries. In light of the understandable doubts about the document's authenticity, I begin with a somewhat detailed account of how it came into my possession. Readers may judge for themselves the veracity of my account and the authenticity of the document.

Chapter I

Origins of the Document

I admit it. I was as suspicious as anyone when I first saw it. In fact, I thought that someone was playing a joke on me. The kind of joke that only middle-age academics, living lives a bit removed from the real word, would get. Even after reading it, for some time I remained as skeptical as many of the scholars and practitioners of Buddhism who are about to read the translation of it that follows. I scoffed at the very notion of a 'lost sutra' of the Buddha.[1] After all, there are 'lost scriptures' of all sorts magically turning up here and there all the time, from the once-hidden *'terma'* texts of the Tibetans[2] to new Christian 'Gospels', to the spooky productions allegedly written by invisible Masters for Madame Blavatsky of the Theosophical Society, to countless others. Yet another scam, I thought, perpetuated on a gullible population of scholars who are desperate for any means to make a name for themselves in the publishing world, lest they forever be denied the college professor's Holy Grail: tenure.

Granted, the Buddhist canon is a large one, with several hundred sutras, or sermons of the Buddha, collected and translated in such a bewildering array of texts, in so many different languages: Pali, Sanskrit, Tibetan, Chinese, Japanese. But like most other spiritual traditions that have survived as established institutions, Buddhism developed a canon, or a (generally) agreed-upon body of texts believed to be the authentic teachings of the Buddha. True, the contents of the canons of the three main branches of Buddhism (Hinayana,[3] Mahayana, and Vajrayana) differ somewhat, with Mahayana and Vajrayana Buddhists each having texts unique to their own tradition. Nonetheless, all agree on what is commonly called the Pali canon: the collection of Hinayana texts, written in Pali, that are universally accepted by all Buddhists to be the actual words of the Buddha, as memorized by his devout disciple Ananda, and recorded around 480 BCE at the first Buddhist Council of Rajagriha. The notion that somehow a document containing the original teachings of the Buddha had been 'lost' for over 2000 years, only to turn up in my hotel room – the hotel room of an obscure, middle-aged religion professor from a tiny rural Pennsylvania college, whose career in academia had been one of mediocrity at best – well, it just seemed completely preposterous.

So how did it happen?

Earlier in the day, like many an anxious assistant professor seeking to build up a case to convince his colleagues that he was deserving of tenure, I had presented a short paper comparing the concept of the self in Zen Buddhism and Soren Kierkegaard at the regional meeting of the American Academy of Religion in Baltimore, Maryland. Regional AAR meetings, in contrast to the national meeting, are definitely a 'second-tier' setting for scholars: a place to present a paper where, given the somewhat sparse attendance and usual lack of prominent names in any field, one can be reasonably assured of making a presentation on just about any topic without receiving any harsh feedback that might, through the rumor mill, make it back to your home college and tenure committee. So in the context of that safe, secure, second-rate scholar-friendly setting, I had once again appeared to speak for a half hour or so on an abstruse topic that few in the audience had ever heard of, and fewer still felt brave enough to offer any challenging questions about.

Having gone through this exercise before, I felt fairly comfortable during my presentation, standing behind the lectern, delivering my prepared remarks with a bit more energy and enthusiasm than was the norm. But in the midst of the presentation, while immersed in the text from which I was reading, I was momentarily distracted by a noise and movement in the rear of the room, near the only entrance door, which, at the beginning of my presentation, had been closed. Glancing quickly at the figure that had just stepped through the door and now stood with his back against the wall, I saw what looked like a short Asian gentleman – probably Chinese, dressed in what appeared to be a monk's robe, clutching a parcel of some sort that was wrapped in what looked like a rather rough burlap-type cloth.

His presence – in a room of fifteen or so stereotypical scholars, all wearing some version of the tweed or corduroy-jacket/oxford cloth button down shirt/khaki pants uniform of the moderately – but only moderately – successful academic – was, to say the least, a bit out of the ordinary in that room. Actually, it was a bit disconcerting, for reasons which, at the time, I really couldn't identify. I just had this vague feeling of a disturbing presence having entered into the room. But like a good scholar, determined to get through the presentation so that I could add another entry to my curriculum vitae, I lowered my head, ignored the presence of the peculiar visitor, and read through the rest of my paper in the rather mechanical manner that partici-pants in regional meetings are all too accustomed to hearing. At the end of the presentation, I looked up, expecting to see the monkish figure, anticipating that as the 'real deal' (someone who *practiced*, rather than merely taught about, Buddhism) he might pose a few challenging questions to me.

But much to my surprise, he was gone, having departed as

3

mysteriously as he had entered.

After a few minutes of mingling with my colleagues, I went up to my room, planning to relax for a few minutes, get changed, and head down to the hotel bar for a quick beer. Upon entering my room, I was taken aback – to say the least – to see a small package on my bed. Even though I had only glanced at the monk and his package in the lecture room for a few brief seconds, I immediately made a connection between the two. The brown, burlap-like wrapping, folded around the contents in a careful but clearly hand-done manner, and tied with a piece of rough brown thread – for some reason that I can't quite explain, I immediately knew that this was the same package that the monk had been holding. My reaction was puzzlement mixed with both fear and excitement: How did he get this into my locked room? Why did he leave it in the room? Why *my* room? Could it be dangerous? Could it be a bomb or some sort of dangerous device, delivered to me in a case of mistaken identity? Could it be some sort of elaborate hoax played on me by colleagues? Of course, I had absolutely no answers to any of those questions, leaving me with just one big "WHAT IS IT?" and an unbearable nervous excitement not unlike a young child on Christmas morning.

I debated my next step: Call security? Open it immediately? Call some colleagues to solicit their advice? After much hesitation, I decided that the best course of action would be no action, or at least no immediate action – best to simply think about it for a bit. For those who are puzzled by such a response I can only say that that's my habitual manner of dealing with a difficult situation: put off a decision by thinking about it for awhile. So I changed into more casual clothes, tucked the package in my briefcase, locked the briefcase and slid it under the bed, and headed to the hotel bar.

In an odd sort of way, I felt some relief at getting out of the room and away from the package – leaving behind the myste-rious and exotic and returning to the world of the ordinary and banal. Once in the lounge, I found a seat at the bar and ordered a beer, hoping to perhaps encounter someone with whom I could watch some good old American football or some other sort of inane, uncontroversial, everyday entertainment for an hour or so. But my intentions were quickly disrupted as, while waiting at the bar for my beer, something caught my eye from a dark corner of the lounge. Glancing into the dim lighting, an uneasy feeling came over me as I saw, looking out of place to a degree that I cannot begin to describe, the Asian monk sitting at a small table, by himself.

As our eyes met, he slowly and gracefully nodded his head, as if to acknowledge that he knew what was already going through my mind. Leaving the beer at the bar, I slowly walked to his table and hesitatingly introduced myself. Given that at this point I was in a state of utter bewilderment, I cannot recall with precision the nature of our 'conversation,' other than to say that it was brief and one-sided. After stammering out my name and making reference to his presence at my presentation and the package found in my room – a rambling, nervous monologue that lasted far too long – realizing that I sounded like a fool, I apologized for my behavior and paused, nervously awaiting his explanation for this bizarre chain of events. Instead, after what seemed to be a silence of several minutes (but in reality was perhaps only a few seconds), he spoke the following friendly but concise reply:

"Dr. Adams, I am pleased to meet you. And I am pleased that you have received my gift. I entrust it to your care, and ask only that you see that it is properly protected and made known to those who would find it of interest. Dunhuang[4] has many secrets. This one has been entrusted to you."

And with that, he rose, bowed slightly, and gracefully walked out of the bar. Dumbfounded, I unfortunately sat in my chair, my head spinning, for a minute or so before getting up and running after him. But he was nowhere to be found. I searched throughout the lobby, outside the hotel, in every conference room. I looked in every stall in every men's bathroom on the first floor. I even made a fool of myself by asking the clerk at the front desk if she had seen a Chinese monk walk by, and, when she stared at me with a puzzled look and said she had not, casting all sense of humility and political correctness and respect for privacy aside, I demanded to know if any Asians were registered at the hotel! That question, of course, confirmed to the poor girl that I was drunk or crazy, and she immediately left the front desk, presumably to go find the manager or security, while I beat a hasty retreat back to my room.

Opening the door to my room, I wondered if the package would still be there. Indeed, part of me hoped that it would not, given the bizarre and mysterious events that had just transpired. Of course, the package was still there. Right where I had left it. With a certain sense of fear and feeling quite foolish, I carefully inspected the room to insure that no one else was there: behind the shower curtain, under the bed, in the closet, all to no avail.

Convinced that I was indeed alone, and that it would be alone that I would have to deal with my mysterious possession, I sat on the bed, placed the package in front of me, carefully untied the string, and unwrapped the burlap packaging. Inside I found what appeared to be a very old, but surprisingly well-preserved scroll. The contents of the scroll were written in Pali, the ancient language of the earliest Buddhist sutras. My knowledge of Pali is quite limited, but I could read the language sufficiently well to translate the title: **Sutra on the Deathbed Reflections of the Buddha**.

My reaction was one of complete bewilderment. The possibility that this was all some sort of elaborate hoax led me to remain calm and composed, pondering the manuscript with the detached objectivity of an academic. But the other possibility, hinted at by the apparent antiquity of the document, the Pali characters filling page after page, and the monk's reference to Dunhuang – the possibility that this might actually be a previously unknown Buddhist sutra, delivered to me for some unfathomable reason by a Buddhist monk, caused me to feel some strange combination of exhilaration and terror: exhilaration that such a rare object could be in my possession, terror over the utter strangeness of it all.

For the sake of brevity and moving the reader on to the actual content of that package, I will briefly summarize what transpired over the next several months. For several days after the conference, I kept the scroll in my possession at all times, even sitting it on the night stand beside my bed when I slept. In order to avoid damage to the frail pages, I intentionally resisted the urge to page through it and explore its contents. Realizing that the nature of my 'gift' was something that would have to be evaluated by others more qualified than myself, over the next several months I sought the opinions of numerous specialists in Pali and Buddhist studies – some academics, some practicing Buddhists, some both. The reactions of various experts to the scroll were remarkably varied – from scorn to virtual veneration, from refusal to even consider it as an authentic sutra to exorbitant offers to purchase the scroll on the spot.

What, then, did I find out about the nature of my little treasure? Basically, two things: first, its antiquity was confirmed. Although carbon dating has not yet been completed, those experts who were willing to examine the document were unanimous in concluding that it was indeed a text that had been produced in the same time period that the canonical Pali texts appeared. However, as for its authenticity, that was another matter. Many refused to even consider the possibility that an original teaching of the Buddha, and particularly one of such a controversial nature, had almost miraculously remained hidden for over twenty centuries.[5] A few were willing to grant that there were a number of intriguing factors that suggested the possibility of its authenticity, but again, given the sutra's controversial content, even those sympathetic experts were reluctant to offer a definitive opinion on the origin of the document.

All of which leads to the challenge posed by the document for the reader: Is it a valid teaching of the Buddha, a sutra whose content is so explosive that it impacts the entire Buddhist canon? Or is it simply a clever forgery? Is it fact, or is it fiction?

This question, for now (and perhaps for the foreseeable future) must be answered by each reader for him/herself. Lacking historical, linguistic or other definitive proof regarding the authenticity of the work, I can only ask each reader to judge accordingly. Some may conclude that this short sutra radically undermines the early Buddhist tradition and challenges their appreciation of the authoritative nature of the Buddha's teachings. Others may see this as a silly piece of fiction that has no impact whatsoever on the great tradition of Buddhism.

I would, however, suggest that even the skeptical reader pause to consider the *content* of this alleged sutra, regardless of its historical origin. For even if the work is the product of someone who lived many years after the Buddha, the issues that it poses and the challenges to traditional Buddhist views that it articulates through the words of the Buddha, may nonetheless present a challenge to certain aspects of the Buddhist dharma that deserve serious consideration, regardless of origin. I ask the reader to read with an open mind and sincerely evaluate the ideas, independent of whom the author might have been.

Chapter 2

Introduction: Buddhism and the Mahaparinirvana Sutra

While it is likely that most readers of this book will already be familiar with Buddhism, for those who are not this chapter provides a very brief summary of the life of the Buddha and his basic teachings, known as the dharma.[6] In addition, and perhaps most importantly for understanding the 'lost' sutra which is found in chapters three through eight, this chapter also provides a brief introduction to the *Mahaparinirvana Sutra*, the canonical text which provides an account of the last days of the Buddha, and the content of which is challenged by the sutra translated here for the first time.

The Life of the Buddha

The person to whom we refer to as the 'Buddha' was born as Siddhartha Gautama around the year 563 BCE, in what is now Nepal.[7] 'Buddha' is actually a title meaning the awakened or enlightened one, and hence this designation does not technically apply to Siddhartha until his Enlightenment around the age of 35. Siddhartha was born into the *kshatriya*, or warrior caste. His father, King Shuddhodana, was a great ruler who hoped that his son would likewise grow up to become a powerful worldly ruler.

Shortly after Siddhartha's birth, Hindu holy men noticed that the young child had the physical signs associated with a *Mahapurusha*, or Great Being. They predicted to his father, King Shuddhodana, that Siddhartha would grow up to become one of two very different kinds of Great Beings: either a great worldy ruler of men, like Shuddodana, or an enlightened holy man, or *sannyasin*. King Shuddhodana was quite familiar with the wandering *sannyasins* who passed through his kingdom: having abandoned all worldly attachments, possessions, and pleasures, they were known for their gaunt bodies, long disheveled hair, ragged clothing, and the practice of remaining in trance-like yogic and meditative states for long periods of time. As a loving father, the King did not want his son to grow up to lead such a harsh life of austerity and deprivation. Consequently, Shuddhodana resolved that he would raise Siddhartha in such a way that he would be shielded from all forms of unhappiness, suffering, and mortality, thereby discouraging him from experiencing any discontent with worldly life and seeking fulfillment in the spiritual life.

The King's plan worked well for almost thirty years, as Siddhartha, living in the sheltered confines of the palace grounds where all of his needs were met, grew up as an indulged king's son, even marrying a beautiful woman and fathering a young son. All was to change, however, around the age of 29, when Siddhartha took a series of unauthorized chariot rides outside the palace grounds, where he was exposed to things that he had never before encountered: aging, sickness, and death. This exposure to the tragic side of life left the prince deeply shaken, revealing to him that the life of pleasure that his father had staged for him was mere illusion. If all beings were subject to aging, sickness, and, ultimately, the annihilation of death, what happiness could one find in worldly pleasures? The answer appeared to Siddhartha in yet another excursion outside the palace grounds, where, for the first time, he saw a *sannyasin*, a holy man who had renounced all wordly pleasures to seek the lasting happiness of spiritual enlightenment.

Convinced that the path of the *sannyasin* was the only source of happiness, Siddhartha resolved that he too would follow this path. One night, when all were sleeping, he quietly left the palace grounds – leaving behind all that he had known and loved, including his wife and son – to embark on the lonely path of the *sannyasin* – the very path that his father had attempted to steer him away from.

For seven years, Siddhartha traveled as a wandering *sannyasin*, studying with several different accomplished teachers, and acquiring the capacity to enter into the deepest states of yogic meditation. And yet, despite these feats of mental concentration, he still did not feel that he had found the key to spiritual enlightenment. Consequently, he left the small group of *sannyasins* with whom he had been traveling and resolved to sit under a tree, in meditation, until such time that he understood the path to spiritual truth and achieved Enlightenment. Various Buddhist texts give differing accounts of the exact events that followed, but all agree that for several days Siddhartha sat in meditation, entering into the four *dhyanas*, or states of meditative absorption. Finally, he achieved a full understanding of reality as it actually is, the source of unhappiness, and the key to achieving happiness through escaping the wheel of rebirth. Siddhartha had achieved Enlightenment: he had become the Buddha.

According to some texts, during his meditation Siddhartha was spiritually assaulted by the god Mara, the tempter, who initially attempted to interrupt Siddhartha's concentration, but, after failing at this and recognizing that the now-Buddha had attained Enlightenment, sought to convince him that the knowledge that he had acquired was so subtle and profound that it would be impossible to communicate it to others. "Why," Mara asked, "waste your time trying to teach others that which they will not be able to comprehend? Why not just let your life end, and enter into the blessed state of nirvana?"

Though tempted to do so, the Buddha was encouraged by other gods to rise from meditation and spread the knowledge that he had gained to others. This is the choice that the Buddha made, beginning a ministry that would last forty five years, as he taught thousands of disciples while wondering across northern India, until his death at age 80.

What, then, did the Buddha teach? What was the content of his Enlightenment? In a sense, Mara was right: the knowledge that the Buddha had acquired was indeed exceedingly subtle and difficult to communicate, full of nuances, utterly new ways of thinking, and paradoxical perspectives. For the sake of brevity, we will highlight the basics of the Buddha's teaching, or dharma, with the understanding that this is indeed only a superficial introduction to a truth whose profundity requires much greater elaboration.

The Four Noble Truths

The first teaching, or sutra, delivered by the Buddha contained what is often understood as the essence of Buddhist teaching: the Four Noble Truths. However, the Four Noble Truths are in turn intimately connected with another Buddhist teaching, the Three Marks of Existence, and indeed many would suggest that the former teaching cannot be understood without reference to the latter.

The Four Noble Truths consist of:

1. The truth of **Duhkha**, or the universality of *unhappiness*
2. The truth of **Samudaya**, or the *origin* of unhappiness in desire, craving, or grasping
3. The truth of **Nirodha**, or *cessation* of unhappiness through the elimination of desire/craving/grasping
4. The truth of **Marga**, or the *Path* to enlightenment and

liberation from rebirth

The first truth, *Duhkha*, declares that *all* aspects of human existence are characterized by pain, suffering, or simply unhappiness. This is the fundamental, uncompromising starting point of the Buddhist worldview. There are the obvious experiences of direct, immediate, obvious pain and suffering that people experience as the result of physical and emotional hurt. However, the Buddha observed that even those things that appear to bring us happiness and pleasure will eventually bring about unhappiness, pain, and sorrow. Youth and good health do not last: they inevitably are transformed into the painful experiences of illness, disease, old age, and ultimately death. Relationships that bring us joy eventually dissolve and leave us lonely or are transformed into centers of conflict, tension, jealousy, betrayal, and anger. Experiences that bring us happiness at one point in our life do not last, becoming transformed into mere repetitive acts of boredom and routine, or in some cases, the source of direct pain and suffering.

The second noble truth, *Samudaya*, establishes that the cause of this universal unhappiness is our ceaseless desire, craving, or grasping, as we attempt to acquire happiness through grasping onto persons, possessions, places, experiences, and even ideas, falsely believing that those ephemeral, constantly changing aspects of reality can provide us with lasting happiness. In a sense, looking for *permanent* happiness by grasping at and becoming attached to *impermanent* aspects of the world is the fundamental existential source of human misery. Indeed, the role of mistaken attachments cannot be over-emphasized. It is not just the grasping at objects of desire that causes unhappiness, but the attachment that we develop toward those objects as a result of the temporary experience of happiness that they provide. Inevitably, however, that sense of happiness fades, and we find ourselves attached to something which, no longer providing us with the happiness that it once did, we now experience with disappointment, anger, resentment, and other negative feelings.

Samudaya has been characterized by a contemporary Western Buddhist as a 'sense of lack,' and the belief that we can fill that sense of lack if we only find the right person, possession, experience, etc.[8] We get caught up in mistakenly thinking along the lines of, "If I only had_____, *then* I would be happy." If I only had the right relationship, the right job, the right income, the right face and body, the right personality, even the right spiritual experience, *then* I would be happy. Of course, this simply leads to a futile and frustrating grasping for and clinging to things that, in a sense, just can't deliver: no conditioned, impermanent reality can deliver the permanent spiritual contentment that all human beings long for.

What then is the solution? According to the third noble truth, the solution is actually quite simple, at least in theory: *Nirodha*, or cessation of desire/grasping/craving. If desire and the subsequent attachments cause unhappiness, then, quite logically, eliminating desire and those desire-generated attachments should lead to the end of unhappiness and the emergence of its opposite, the joy of spiritual enlightenment. Of course, that prescription for happiness needs to be fleshed out a bit, and there's the rub: it's easy to say that one can acquire true happiness by eliminating desire, but doing so is quite another matter. In a sense, it amounts to a monumental task of reversing much of what seems to be built into our nature and taught to us virtually from birth. Fortunately, the Buddha provides some specifics regarding how to eliminate desire, and that leads to the final noble truth of the *Marga*, or Path.

More specifically, the Buddha taught that desire could be eliminated, unhappiness conquered, and spiritual enlightenment achieved through diligently following the Eightfold Path, consisting of right views, right intentions, right speech, right conduct, right livelihood, right effort, right mindfulness, and right concentration.

The first step on the Path, right views, refers to an accurate and honest understanding of the nature of reality as it truly is. In a sense, right views function as the foundation for all of the other steps on the Path. We will examine the details of right views when we examine the Three Marks of Existence below.

The second step, right intentions, is fairly self-explanatory: one should follow the Path with sincere intentions, devoid of ego, pride, etc.

The next three steps (right speech, conduct, and livelihood) constitute the ethical elements of the path, and, in general, include fairly universal prescriptions for living a moral life, with additional requirements set down for those who pursue a monastic lifestyle.

Right effort reflects the difficulty of the Path: one must be strenuously devoted to following the Path over a long period of time. Spiritual enlightenment, from a Buddhist perspective, is not something that one achieves overnight.

Most of the above elements of the Eightfold Path are similar to the path found in all of the world's major religious traditions. What makes Buddhism distinctive (aside from the 'Right Views' which we will cover shortly) are the last two steps of the Path: right mindfulness (*sati*) and right concentration (*samadhi*). Both *sati* and *samadhi* are terms that are used in the Buddhist tradition to express multiple meanings, and hence it is a bit tricky to pin down, in the span of a short summary, the precise content of these steps.

In a general sense, *sati*, or mindfulness, refers to a mind that is always aware of all aspects of its operations and surroundings. The truly mindful person is one who is supremely alert at all times, aware of his body, thoughts, feelings, and perceptions. Mindfulness allows one to be in control of one's mental life, rather than being pulled in various directions by the constant, habitual, craving and desire.

Both mindfulness and the last step on the Path, *samadhi*, are cultivated through the practice of meditation. Buddhist meditation is practiced quite differently by the various schools of the tradition, but in general, it is accurate to say that *samadhi* refers to the indescribable state of deep, peaceful concentration that is the end-state of meditative practice and the portal to enlightenment. 'Concentration' is clearly too prosaic of a word to do the term justice: this is indeed an exceedingly rare type of concentration, a state of consciousness acquired by a spiritual elite through years of intense meditative practice.

The Eightfold Path is sometime classified according to three categories: 1) *Sila*, or morality (consisting of right speech, conduct, and livelihood); 2) *Samadhi*, or mental discipline (consisting of mindfulness and concentration); and 3) *Prajna*, or wisdom (consisting of right intentions and, most, importantly, right views). In a sense, Buddhist practice is both rooted in and culminates in the acquisition of right views, or an understanding of reality as it is. Hence, enlightenment is not simply an empty state of blissful trance, but rather an alert, fully conscious understanding of the true nature of reality, and this liberating knowledge is the basis of enlightenment and freedom from the dreaded wheel of rebirth.

What, then, constitutes right views, or a true understanding of reality as it is? Once again, we find this articulated quite clearly by the Buddha when he describes the Three Marks of Existence (*trilakshana*), those being impermanence, suffering, and no-self.

The first mark, or characteristic, of the nature of reality is *Duhkha*, or universal unhappiness or suffering. This, of course, is also the first of the Four Noble Truths, and hence we have already covered its basic meaning and implications.

However, the universality of suffering is intimately related to the second mark of existence which we will examine: impermanence, or *Anitya*. In a sense, the Buddhist emphasis on universal impermanence is the belief about the nature of reality that serves as the foundation stone for all other Buddhist beliefs, and hence it requires careful consideration. The Buddha asserts that everything in the world in which we live is in a constant state of change, and hence its condition at any given moment is impermanent. This assertion of impermanence is uncompromising: *everything* is impermanent – things, places, experiences, even our very self (which leads to the third mark of existence, examined below). In a sense, the Buddha is repudiating the comfortable fantasy world that his father had constructed (a version of which all of us construct in various ways) to prevent him from seeking spiritual enlightenment: the enlightened Siddhartha saw that, however pleasurable his life was within the palace grounds, *everything* that brought him happiness would eventually change, and indeed, decay and, if living, die.

This existential insight is essential to understanding the early Buddhist worldview. The Buddha broke away from the myth that we build up around ourselves, finding pleasure in various aspects of life without facing the reality that those sources of happiness will change and disappear, as will the happiness that derives from them. In a sense, we are constantly chasing after new sources of happiness because we cannot face the existential terror of admitting that nothing will last, leaving us in the end with....what? That uncertainty is spiritually devastating, and the Buddha recognized that we spend our entire lives trying to evade it by immersing ourselves in one temporary fix of happiness after the other, not taking the time to recognize that at some point that hopeless pursuit will come to an end[9].

The truth of the impermanence of all things is also the basis for the universality of unhappiness, or suffering. Given that everything in the world is characterized by impermanence, anything that we become attached to as a source of happiness, be it a person, place, thing, experience – truly anything - will at some point no longer be there to provide that happiness. In essence, by becoming attached to anything, we set ourselves up for inevitable unhappiness, since the object of our attachment will eventually be gone. Craving for and attachment to something that is impermanent cannot lead to permanent, abiding happiness, and given that all things are impermanent, it follows that no thing can lead to such happiness.

The third of the three marks of existence is *anatman*, or no-self. This doctrine[10] states there is no permanent, abiding entity which we can refer to as our self. We are deluded when we think that a temporary aggregate or collection of elements which hang together over the span of several decades of a human life constitute some sort of permanent entity, referred to as a self or soul (*atman*). The Buddha offers many and sometimes puzzling teachings about the truth of no-self, but perhaps the easiest way to understand *anatman* is through the Buddha's use of the wheel analogy. A wheel consists of a hub, spokes, and rim. But when we take away those constituent parts, when we remove the hub, spokes, and rim, where is the wheel? Of course, there is no wheel once the parts are removed, since 'wheel' is simply a word or name used to designate what is in essence an abstract concept, namely that of a united hub, spokes, and rim.

Using the wheel example, the Buddha declares that what we think is our 'self' is merely the temporary hanging together of various psychophysical elements, known as the five *skandhas*, or aggregates. Specifically, when form (body), thoughts, feelings/perceptions, dispositions, and consciousness coalesce and stay together over an extended time period, we come to mistakenly believe that there exists a 'self' which is the center of these five elements. In reality, 'self' is merely a fictional designation, which is seen by the fact that when we remove the form, thoughts, feelings, dispositions, and consciousness, what is left? Nothing! In other words, as with the wheel, once the parts are removed, the illusory nature of the reified entity, be it a wheel or self, becomes apparent.

Anatman is a key element of Buddhism, and perhaps the

concept that most significantly separates it from not only the Indic religious traditions out of which Buddhism emerged but, even more radically, from all religious traditions. While other religions are rooted in the promise of some sort of eternal personal blessedness that is the prize at the end of the spiritual quest, Buddhism takes what appears to be a somewhat contrarian position, suggesting that belief in a self is an illusion, and an illusion that must be cast aside to achieve spiritual enlightenment.

Of course, this raises some challenging questions: If there is no self, then what exactly am I? If enlightenment consists in the discovery that my self will be annihilated once my body dies and my mental faculties dissipate, then what is the appeal of the spiritual path? This is perhaps the most vexing issue in Buddhist thought, and the Buddha himself carefully avoided providing a direct answer to these questions. His followers were certainly not averse to asking him for clarification on such an important issue, but the Buddha responded that such questions were not conducive to edification, or the knowledge leading to enlightenment. At times, he asserts that while the essentialist position (that the self exists and is eternal) is not true, likewise the annihilationist position (that the self ceases to exist at death) is also not true[11]. Of course, one might argue here that one or the other must be true: this seems to be something of an either-or issue. The Buddha partially deals with this by suggesting that there are certain truths that are simply too profound for the limited human intellect to comprehend, and that instead of wasting time at useless, unproductive metaphysical speculation, one should faithfully follow the practice that is guaranteed to lead to supreme happiness, or nirvana. The precise nature of that nirvana and the role of or non-role of the self in nirvana, are issues that simply cannot be articulated in language, and hence the spiritual seeker is advised to avoid frittering away time and energy on useless speculation and focus on the knowable and achievable elements that lead to freedom from suffering and true happiness[12].

One may or may not find the Buddha's position on the nature of the self to be convincing, but that's somewhat beside the point. For our purposes in understanding what was taught by the Buddha, we simply need to acknowledge that the Buddha taught the doctrine of *anatman* – as perplexing and elusive as it might be.

The Buddhist path, then, can be summarized as a quest, through the practice of morality, meditation and the acquisition of wisdom (as in the Three Marks of Existence) which leads to the cessation of suffering through the gradual elimination of craving and its resultant attachments, eventually producing in the practitioner a state of mind which is utterly free from unhappiness.

Ananda and the Mahaparinirvana Sutra

Of the thousands of converts who accepted the dharma of the Buddha and joined the *Sangha*, or community of Buddhist monks, as a full-time follower of the teacher, several rose to prominent status (Shariputra, Upali, Mahakashyapa, Anuruddha, for example), but perhaps none were closer to the Buddha than Ananda, the most well-known of his many disciples. Ananda plays a key role in the *Mahaparinirvana Sutra*, and, as we shall see, he is the 'author/recorder' of the *Deathbed Sutra* which follows.

A cousin of the Buddha, Ananda grew up with the young Siddhartha in the city of Kapilavastu. After Siddhartha's Enlightenment and the beginning of his ministry as the Buddha, Ananda became a disciple, accepting the dharma and becoming a monk at the age of 37. When the Buddha reached age 55, he announced to the Sangha that he was in need of an *upatthaka*, or personal attendant, a position which was awarded to Ananda in recognition of his devotion to the dharma and commitment to the Buddha.

Ananda remained the Buddha's attendant for 25 years, and, as described in the *Mahaparinirvana Sutra*, was at his side when he died. As such, perhaps no one was on more intimate terms with the Buddha than Ananda. As the Buddha's attendant, Ananda was responsible for a wide range of mundane tasks devoted to the personal needs of the Buddha, such as bringing water the Buddha used for washing his face, finding wood for brushing his teeth, arranging the Buddha's seat, fanning him, sweeping his living space, mending his robes, etc. Each night Ananda slept near the Buddha so as to be immediately available to respond to his needs. Ananda also acquired a somewhat authoritative role within the Sangha: he was responsible for summoning the monks together when the Buddha was prepared to deliver a message, at times other monks sought Ananda for clarification of the Buddha's teachings, and on occasions when the Buddha was ill he entrusted Ananda with the responsibility of delivering his teaching to the Sangha.

But above all else, Ananda was renowned for his extraordinary memory. Consequently, at the first Buddhist Council, held in Rajagriha shortly after the Buddha's death, Ananda is said to have recited from memory 82,000 of the Buddha's teachings, or sutras. Ananda's memorized recitation led to the establishment of the major part of the Buddhist canon, the collection of teachings known as the Sutra Basket. For his remarkable capacity to remember the Buddha's teachings, he was given the title of 'Guardian of the Dharma.'[13]

The most extensive canonical description of the close relationship between the Buddha and Ananda is found in the *Mahaparinirvana Sutra*,[14] which describes the final weeks of the life of the Buddha. The title, *mahaparinirvana*, can be translated as 'great final nirvana.' In Buddhist teaching, one can achieve the state of nirvana 'with or without remainder,' meaning with or without residual karma. A Buddhist who has achieved nirvana but still has accumulated karma that needs to be played out, will experience another rebirth in order to allow that karmic process to reach its completion. However, one who has achieved nirvana 'without remainder' has no residual karma, and hence will not be reborn again. This final achievement of nirvana with the assurance of no rebirths is known as the *mahaparinirvana*.

In the *Mahaparinirvana Sutra*, the Buddha, accompanied by his long-time personal attendant, Ananda, travels to multiple places, teaching the dharma along the way to large groups, small groups, and individual disciples, both monastic and lay. These teachings do not represent anything new, but rather are a recapitulation of previous sutras. In a sense, the Sutra seems to describe a 'farewell tour' of the Buddha, who covers a broad territory while reminding his followers about key elements of the dharma that he has taught over the previous four decades.

The Sutra ends with the death of the Buddha and his presumed entrance into nirvana. After eating a meal prepared by a lay follower, the Buddha becomes extremely ill, and eventually dies, teaching to the very end as reflected in the 'deathbed scene' which leads to his actual passing. The Sutra closes with the cremation of the Buddha's body and the distribution of its remains, which become sacred relics.

It should be noted that there is nothing surprising or disturbing about the *Mahaparinirvana Sutra*. As indicated above, the teachings consist of very basic dharma which has previously been taught by the Buddha, and, the events, including the Buddha's death, are quite unremarkable.

It is in the context of the unremarkable nature of the *Mahaparinirvana Sutra* that the lost *Deathbed Sutra* must be read, for, as will become apparent, the lost sutra is anything but unremarkable, and calls into question not only the events of that final night but, in a sense, the very nature of the dharma itself.

Chapter 3

Ananda's Preface

I, Ananda, attendant to Siddhartha Gautama, the Buddha, do attest to the veracity of the following account of the last night of the Blessed One. In presenting this account, I acknowledge its discrepancies with the *Mahaparinirvana Sutra*. Hence, I affirm that the following account of that final night is true, and that the account previously given in the *Mahaparinirvana Sutra* is, regrettably, inaccurate. For those whom I offend, I ask forgiveness.

These past ten years, since the Buddha's passing – how can I describe the misery that I have suffered within, while to the world of fellow monks I have maintained the appearance of one who has conquered all sorrow. Oh such a false, hypocritical appearance I have put on, and oh how it has tormented me inside. Living beside my fellow monks, meditating together, traveling with them to the village for alms, maintaining the buildings and grounds, listening together to the teachings of the Buddha, and joining with them, side by side, in the countless everyday activities, conversations, gestures, and smiles that make for a day in the Sangha. All the while smiling on the outside, while wasting away from guilt on the inside.

I am called by my fellow monks the "Guardian of the Dharma." Blessed with the ability to recall everything that I hear, I memorized over 80,000 of the Blessed One's teachings, and recited them all, without error – not even in a single syllable – at the council of Rajagriha. It was through my words that the words of the master were passed on and given lasting form in the canon of the Basket of Sutras. And yet, how I curse this ability of mine! It was to me that the monks looked for preservation of the words of the Buddha, and every word was indeed perfectly etched inside my mind. But not only the 82,000 sermons that I recited at Rajagriha,[15] the ones that reflected the dharma that all looked upon with reverence and awe, the teaching aptly described as "lovely in the beginning, lovely in the middle, and lovely in the end" ...but also those final words, the last teaching, given only to me, on the night of his death. Indeed, not a teaching so much as a confession. A confession of regret, a confession of confusion, a confession of expiation. And for all those years, with that final conversation burning in my heart and mind, I had to keep silent. For if I had spoken about that final teaching, the authority of the Blessed One, rooted in the assurance of his Enlightenment, would have been shattered. I did not have the courage to destroy the wonderful community that his words had built. I did not have the courage to destroy the miraculous faith that had pervaded the land, transforming men of hatred into men of compassion, bringing peace to lands weary of war, bringing hope of a path to happiness for those weary of the pain and misery of ordinary human life.

Or perhaps I ascribe too lofty a motive to my silence. Perhaps I was simply afraid that no one would believe me. That I would be ostracized (yet once again[16]) by my fellow monks. That I would be excommunicated from the Sangha, and turned away from the life that I so dearly loved. Perhaps it would have been better that way: to simply tell the truth, recite the events of that final night, let the leaders of the Sangha revile and humiliate me with their scornful disbelief, and then quietly go away, allowing them to think of those final words of the Buddha as nothing more than a fantasy from the crazed mind of Ananda. Perhaps that would have been best. But speculating on my motive is pointless now: in setting down the words that follow, I have done what needs to be done, and I will accept the consequences, however harsh and humiliating, with equanimity.

I have called what follows a 'sutra,' but it is not a sutra in the traditional sense of the word. That is to say, it is not limited to the words of the Buddha. Certainly it includes the Blessed One's words, but it also includes my own narration of the setting and context in which the conversation – that terrible, shattering conversation – took place between him and myself on the final night of his earthly existence as Siddhartha Gautama. I have designated this account as a sutra in deference to what I believe is the importance of that conversation, which, in a sense, was the final teaching of the Buddha. Not 'only' the final teaching, but, in a sense, the teaching which transforms the meaning of everything that he taught before that fateful night. For those who feel that I am not justified in designating as a 'sutra' an account which includes many of my own words, I ask only that they try to understand my intent for doing so, and humbly ask for their forgiveness.

For those unfamiliar with the *Mahaparinirvana Sutra*, I shall briefly describe the events that led up to that final, fateful, agonizing night with my Master.

For several weeks we had been touring the land, stopping at various sites where the Buddha had previously taught and established the dharma. On many occasions he spoke to large groups of monks, on some occasions he spoke to just a single person, sometimes a follower of the dharma, at other times a doubter who became converted to the dharma by the words of the Blessed One.

I felt a certain vague foreboding about this journey, although

I could not quite identify the cause of my worry. However, I knew that something was seriously wrong when, after eating food prepared by Ambapali, benefactor of the Mango Grove outside Veshali, the Buddha became gravely ill and declared, "Now I am frail, Ananda, old, aged, far gone in years. This is my eightieth year, and my life is spent. Even as an old cart, Ananda, is held together with much difficulty, so the body of the Tathagata[17] is kept going only with supports."[18]

The following day, my fears were confirmed when the Buddha pronounced, without equivocation, that that day he had renounced the will to live, and that in three months he would pass from this embodied existence.

Still, despite the agonizing pain that he was constantly enduring, and as befitting one who had freed himself from all attachments to the realm of form, the Blessed One continued to travel and teach, visiting monks at several settlements before coming to Pava. Reaching the Mango Grove at Pava, once again, after eating a meal, the Buddha became gravely ill, and yet still he insisted on pressing onward to Kushinara, where we settled for the night in the Sala Grove of the Malla clan. And it was here that the events of the last night in the life of this venerable being were to unfold, as it was here that I engaged in that final shocking conversation with my Master which is recounted below.

Declaring that "I am weary, Ananda, and want to lie down,"[19] the Buddha reclined in his traditional sleeping position, the lion's posture. I noticed that his skin had changed, with a radiant quality emanating from his entire body. After kindly thanking me for my years of service and commending me for my commitment to the dharma, the Blessed One gave instructions for the disposition of his corpse. I was indescribably saddened by the growing awareness that this would indeed be the final earthly night in the company of my Master and Teacher. Yet even to the end, and despite his great pain, he thought only of the welfare of others, as he called for a gathering of the local monks, to whom he

delivered his final sermon, a concise summary of the funda-
mentals of the dharma, after which he declared that he would
pass during the night.

And now we come to the difficult part, the part which I would
give a thousand lives to undo, but the part which, for the sake of
being a true chronicler of the words of the Buddha, I must
communicate before I too pass on. In proceeding further with
this account, first I must again take time to beg for the
forgiveness of both those whom I have misled by my earlier
account of my final hours with the Buddha and those to whom I
will bring great turmoil by this revised, but true account of those
final, traumatic hours.

As the hours of that fateful night passed, the Blessed One,
lying in the Lion's Position, displayed no movement, and his
breathing slowed to the point where I feared that he had died.
Staring at my dying Master's still body, I felt a deep sense of
sadness at the thought of never again hearing his voice and the
wise words of the dharma. My Master and friend, for forty years!
Even though I confidently embraced the dharma, knowing that
all sentient beings are impermanent and knowing that the bliss
of nirvana into which the Buddha was about to enter was indeed
cause for great joy, I nonetheless felt deeply despondent and
struggled greatly to not wail in despair and disturb the Blessed
One's deep slumber into nirvana.

But then, in the third watch of the night, with the smooth,
controlled movement of the moon rising above the horizon, to
my utter astonishment, the body of the Buddha slowly rose from
the reclining position. Calmly, and with the graceful deliber-
ateness of movement found only in one who has achieved the
constant Mindfulness that comes with Enlightenment, the
Blessed One assumed the full lotus position. Such a perfect
position, radiating control and equanimity! What a joy it was to
see the Master assume this position again, bringing back those
days before his illness had set in. Speaking while in deep

samadhi, he began to describe the wonderful nature of the experience acquired through meditation:

"Oh Ananda, it is like floating on a calm, glass-like ocean, free of the slightest ripple of worry, anxiety, fear, craving, or any other affliction.

"But then, it becomes something even more sublime: it is like *being* the ocean, upon which no self floats, for there is no separate self, as indeed there is no separate ocean. There is just the pure bliss of consciousness, or mind, or spirit – many words for that which is beyond description.

"In the forty years of my ministry, Ananda, I have said little about this experience, for words are not worthy to convey something so sublime. Any word is misleading, and hence I have chosen to strive for silence, only pointing the way to the experience itself. Through the Tathagata's spiritual eye I can see that in the future, many will try to use the written word to describe the indescribable. Some will be profoundly skillful at the use of words, and yet even so, they will not come close to describing that which I have come to experience in the bliss of samadhi."

Oh, how I was thrilled to hear the Master speak the dharma again! And for a moment, I held out hope that, despite his claim that his death was approaching, he had decided, as was his power to do, to extend his embodied existence a while longer for the sake of his devotees and those who had not yet heard the dharma.

And then... I do not know how to convey the shock of what I was about to see. I, Ananda, the personal attendant of the Buddha for over twenty-five years, had seen many marvelous and wondrous things flow from the words and actions of the Blessed One. Earthquakes, flowers falling from the sky, delicious fragrances filling the air, levitating bodies floating in mid-air.

And yet, what I now witnessed was no cosmic event, and yet, with no doubt whatsoever, was the most profound moment that I ever observed: The Buddha wept.

A tear formed in the corner of his left eye, then fell down his unmoving cheek. Then both eyes filled with tears, and slowly more tears trickled down his still immobile face. I cannot begin to describe the inconceivable nature of what I was witnessing: the motionless lotus-positioned body, supporting the face of a person I hardly recognized! And his skin, so radiant just hours earlier, had now acquired a pallid color, as that of one who is paralyzed by a deep fear. Even his posture, while remaining in the lotus position, seemed to lose its strength and firmness, almost as if his whole being was about to wilt and collapse.

How could this be? Was I dreaming? Was I being deceived by the tempter, Mara? No, for I had progressed far enough in my meditative practice to always differentiate between the dream and wakeful states, and my progress had resulted in immunity from the temptations of the evil one. Yes, I thought, this experience is real!

I remained speechless, dumbfounded by this utter transformation of the being who had been unchanging for decades. In shock and humility, like a bewildered child, I simply stared until he again spoke – this time with a sadness in his voice such as has never been heard from the mouth of a man, uttering words that pierced my heart, words which even today echo in my mind as if they were being uttered at this very moment, words which I would give anything to expel from my distraught mind.

Chapter 4

The Buddha's Confession

"Oh Ananda, oh Ananda." And then followed a long pause which seemed to last forever, filled with a heavy, ominous, dreadful silence. "Forgive me, for I have not spoken the truth."

I stared in shock and disbelief, my world crumbling around me, waiting for the Buddha to say something that would negate those words. But such was not to come, as I already knew in my heart by observing, indeed being drenched with, the unspeakable sorrow that pervaded his entire being: each word, each gesture, the look in his profoundly saddened eyes.

"Oh Ananda, please forgive me for what I have done."

The Blessed One asking *me* for forgiveness! What an absurdity. Surely the nature of this conversation would change in a moment, with the Buddha revealing that he was speaking in jest, or using such words for the sake of teaching a parable. Surely this was the Blessed One again teaching through the use of skillful means.[20] No, it simply could not be the case that the World-Honored One, the greatest, wisest, most compassionate person who existed in the realm of time and space could utter such remarks! And yet, there was no retraction. There was no putting the words into a harmless context. There was only more of the same...more words uttered with a depth of sadness, guilt, and regret that was so profound that it seemed as if the Earth itself was trembling. In shock and fear, with my spirit collapsed, my spine bent forward and body drooping, I listened...

"Oh Ananda. It is a terrible, terrible thing that I have done. It is an unforgiveable thing that I have done. I am deserving of a thousand lives in the deepest realm of the hells.[21] Oh Ananda, I am filled with such despair, a despair which verily is a sickness unto death. Would that I could die, and escape the shame that now pervades my being."

And with that, the Blessed One's body slumped forward and a great sigh of agony came forth from the depths of his spirit.

"But Master, what you say bewilders me. Surely you are jesting with me – perhaps a final joke with me, before you pass into the bliss of final nirvana? Or perhaps you are testing me, testing to see if I will remain by your side even when you feign to have been overcome by madness. Or could it be the case that the Blessed One's illness has infected the brain, and he knows not the meaning of the words that come forth from his mouth? Oh beloved Siddhartha, please tell me that what is happening in front of my eyes is not what it appears to be!"

"Ananda, please forgive me. Forgive me twice: for the pain that I am causing you this very evening by offering my confession to you, but even more so, for the pain that my errant teachings have caused you over the past decades."

"But the Blessed One has caused Ananda no pain. To the contrary, you have given me the dharma, which has brought a deep and abiding happiness that has freed me from the ills of the world and set me on the path to nirvana."

"No!" exclaimed the Buddha. And with this utterance, it seemed as if the entire world shook. Never, no never, had I seen my Master utter a single word in anger, not even when others within the Sangha maliciously schemed against him.[22]

"Ananda, do not credit me with anything. For what you think

has been sweet fruit fed to you through my words has actually been foul, rotten, poisonous meat. You think that I have given you soul-soothing medicine, when in fact the dharma that I have taught has filled you with poison. The rays of wisdom which you believe have cast light on your path to Enlightenment have been like lanterns leading you unknowingly down a path that leads to...I know not what, but certainly not to Enlightenment. I have said of the enlightened Tathagata that he is one who teaches the dharma good in the beginning, good in the middle, and good in the end,[23] but such is not the case for what I have taught the Sangha during these many years. Oh! May my final words tonight undo the terrible harm that I have done – may my teaching of the dharma be good at least in the end."

With those words, the Buddha paused, and his entire being seemed to deflate. Had he died, while still sitting up? Had he entered samadhi? And at the same time, my own being – I cannot quite describe the agony that I experienced: part of me still refusing to believe the reality of what I was perceiving, part of me feeling like my entire world was shattered, feeling as though I was dangling on the edge of an abyss of meaninglessness. But in a few seconds, the Buddha again opened his still tearful eyes, wearily raised his head with great effort, and continued to speak, this time in halting words which I could barely hear.

"Oh Ananda, for over forty years I have traveled across the land, teaching my dharma to all who would hear. I traveled through many territories. I have taught men of all castes, monks and householders, followers of the gods and followers of none, wealthy men of the world and gaunt ascetics and yogis. I have taught countless strangers, but I also have brought into my fold many members of my family and my father's court: stranger and kin alike have received the dharma. Those who have been shunned by other teachers – women and people of the lower caste – with them I have shared the dharma as openly as with the most wealthy and powerful Brahmins. Ananda, how many thousands upon thousands have listened to my words, accepted their truth, and changed their lives to live in accord with my dharma? Many, many thousand, indeed. In the country, in the city, in the forest, in palaces, in ascetics' crude caves, in humble dwellings and in great estates. Yes, Ananda, the influence of my teaching has been profound, spreading a new dharma across the land. How many princes have donated lands, upon which have been built thriving monasteries, filled with monks pursuing the path I have taught? And how many householders are leading a life in accordance with my dharma in the hope that they will be reborn in a new life when they too can take the robe and bowl[24] and pursue the dharma as a bhikshu?[25] Thousands Ananda, yes thousands! Thousands and thousands whom I have deceived! Thousands and thousands whom I have misled! Thousands and thousands whose forgiveness I must earn before being released from the burning hell into which my being shall shortly enter!

"Ananda, what I have taught is in error! What I have taught is not the true dharma! What I have taught has unnecessarily caused many good people to walk down a path which will not lead them to the blessedness which they seek. Oh Ananda, I have been a deceiver!"

I continued to sit there in a state of profound shock. There are no words to describe the depth of that shock. I will not even attempt to do so. I will simply recount the words that the Blessed One continued to utter.

He paused. It seemed as if this first burst of words, however troubling they were to me, had given him some relief. It is said that confession is a good medicine for both spirit and the body. Believing that he had confessed (although the very notion of the perfect Enlightened One having to confess anything made no sense to me at all, and the notion of him confessing to *me* was utterly absurd), the Buddha seemed to regain his composure slightly. His body was a bit more erect. The tears in his eyes were gone. And when he spoke again, it was with greater steadiness – though still full of that profound sense of sorrow and despair.

"Ananda, tonight I will reveal to you the errors that I have made, in the hope that you can spread my parting words throughout the land and, over time, undo the harm that I have done. For many years I have known, in the recesses of my mind, that something was wrong with the dharma that I was teaching. True, it brought a certain kind of peaceful happiness to many, and as such it was good medicine to those who suffered from unhappiness. And yet...and yet, there was this nagging sense that something about the teaching was just not quite right. And this uneasiness was with me for many years. It is true that after my experience of what they call "enlightenment" at Uruvela some four decades ago, I was overcome by the rapturous bliss of that blessed Nirvanic state. And yet, I recall that less than a year after my Enlightenment, while I was gaining followers and building the Sangha, the seeds of doubt began to form.

"But it was a subtle doubt, Ananda. And for that reason, I was able to tuck it away in a far corner of my mind and ignore it...for most of the time. But every now and then – as, for instance, when my son, Rahula, joined the Sangha[26]– that doubt, which was always growing while hidden in the recesses of my heart, as if feeding on my denial of its existence, emerged again, each time with renewed strength, each time coming closer to gaining victory over the meditative equanimity that I had achieved. But my power of concentration was great, and I kept the doubt imprisoned, hidden so deeply in my heart that for long periods of time, I was barely aware of its existence.

"Indeed, Ananda, when the Tathagata assumed the Lion's Position to recline for the final time this evening, he fully expected to pass quietly and peacefully into his Parinirvana. But the awareness of one's impending death – even for one such as myself who has acquired the assurance of enlightenment and liberation from rebirth in the painful realm of samsara – does strange things to a person. Things long hidden in the heart are freed to arise to consciousness as the mind begins to let go – such I have learned this very evening. And hence, while in deep slumber and on the verge of passing on from this woeful transient existence, that which I had hidden for so long burst forth to confront me, refusing to be set aside, demanding its rightful place in the forefront of my mind, and in doing so, shattering the inner peace that I had worked so many years to cultivate.

"And tonight, Ananda, before I take final leave of this realm of suffering and impermanence, this world of greed, delusion, and hatred,[27] I will confess to you my error, so that you may teach it to others. But it is an error that is exceedingly subtle, and precisely because of its subtlety, it weighs heavily on me to even make an effort to describe that error to you.

"Oh Ananda, I am reminded of another occasion when the subtlety of wisdom I had gained was such that I feared the burden of trying to communicate it to others. Surely, Ananda, you recall my encounter with the tempter, Mara.[28] While sitting under the Bodhi tree, intent on remaining in deep meditation until I achieved Enlightenment, I was approached by Mara with temptations of many kinds – efforts to frighten me with his hordes of warriors, efforts to seduce me with his beautiful daughters, all designed to distract me from my resolve to achieve Enlightenment. Unsuccessful at that effort, he approached me again, this time after my Enlightenment but before arising from meditation. In this second attack he sought to persuade me that the truth which I had discovered was of such a deep and subtle nature that I could have no hope of communicating that truth to other sentient beings for the sake of their own liberation. I confess that at that time my confidence wavered, and I considered following the path that Mara recommended: entering into my Parinirvana, content with the knowledge that I had gained, the knowledge that would free me

35

from rebirth. I was deeply swayed by Mara's argument that the deep and subtle nature of the dharma that I had acquired was something beyond my capacity to explain to others, and hence I thought: What is the purpose of my continued existence, now that I have found the path to freedom from rebirth but cannot teach that path to others? Why should I delay my entry into the bliss of Parinirvana?

"But, of course, the gods intervened, imploring me to disregard the counsel of the untrustworthy Mara, and to rise and teach the dharma to all who would listen. And as you know, Ananda, I took the advice of the gods, rose from my meditation, and embarked on the beginning of what has become my teaching ministry of forty-five years, during which time I have taught the dharma, as I understood it, to thousands and thousands.

"Yet throughout those years I was constantly aware of the infinitely subtle nature of that liberating truth that I was attempting to teach, and the constant danger of communicating such subtle truth in a manner that was not accurate. It was like walking on a razor's edge of truth, so easy to fall off the edge by just the slightest loss of balance, plunging from the most sublime truth to the most dangerous error with just the slightest slip of the tongue, just the slightest error in choosing the wrong word to express the inexpressible. Surely you remember my conversation with Malunkyaputta, who presented a series of questions to me regarding such metaphysical issues as the origin of the world, the nature of the self, the relationship of the self to the body, and the destiny of the self after death. Do you recall how I responded to Malunkyaputta's questions? I declared that if I attempted to answers such questions – questions whose answers are found in the realm of profound depth, subtlety, and mystery – it would take more than an entire lifetime to adequately explain the answer to such questions. Malunkyaputta would die before the Tathagata could complete the explanation of such deep truths about the nature of things.[29]

"So throughout the many years in which I taught the dharma, the fear of teaching wrongly was ever present. And tonight, Ananda, terror and regret pour through me, for I fear that Mara was right! The truth that was revealed to me on the night of my Enlightenment was indeed more profound and subtle than words could express, and in trying to teach that truth to others I have misled them. I have brought some measure of happiness to those who suffer, but only at a great and unnecessary price. If only I had remained silent! But tonight, Ananda, I shall undo my error. I shall conquer Mara at last. I shall correct the dharma and present it to you as a parting gift and act of penance. Accept it, my friend, with gladness."

Chapter 5

The Final Teaching: Attachment and Love

"Let me begin, Ananda, by going back to the event that began my search for Enlightenment. It is a story you know well, but one that I will recite in a different light from what you have heard. It is known as the Great Renunciation, but in a sense I believe that it would be more aptly called the Great Shame, or the Great Mistake. As you know, for almost the first three decades of my life, I had led a privileged life as a prince. My father, King Shuddhodana, had provided me with the best of everything. I was young, strong, handsome, married to a beautiful woman who loved me deeply, and the proud father of a young son who adored me. Still, I was keenly aware of the transient nature of this worldly happiness which surrounds us, and my mind incessantly sought a deeper meaning in life. Surely, I thought, there must be a path to a knowledge that would liberate one from all unhappiness and reveal the true nature of things. I had seen the wandering sannyasins, who seemed to be seeking this same wisdom. And hence, at the age of twenty-nine, when my son Rahula was only seven years old, one night when everyone in the palace was sleeping, I quietly left it all behind, to embark on the quest that several years later culminated in my Enlightenment.

"This story is told many times, Ananda, by members of the Sangha, who portray me as a hero for giving up worldly pleasures for the sake of the spiritual quest. And yet, looking back, I cannot help but think that in a certain sense my actions were both cowardly and cruel. What terrible grief I brought to my wife, my child, my father! Was it not a selfish act on my part to leave them with no explanation? Was it not a selfish act to abandon my duties as a son, husband, and father? Does the pursuit of wisdom justify the abandonment of those to whom one is dear? At that time, I did indeed believe that there was a higher life, and that the nature of that higher life justified renunciation of all worldly attachments. And as I acquired a following and taught the dharma, I taught ideas that justified such an act of abandonment. I taught that attachment to all transient phenomena, which of course would include attachment to people, must be rejected in order to achieve the wisdom that liberates.

"But now, Ananda, I recognize that I was mistaken. I recognize that the love that exists between father and son, between husband and wife, between any two human beings who genuinely care about each other, is something very precious and rare. It is something that should be treasured and nurtured, not something that must be abandoned in order to pursue the spiritual path. I have often taught, Ananda, that a human birth is a precious event that one should treasure, since no other birth provides the opportunity for enlightenment and liberation. But just as a human birth is a precious gift, so too are the many wonderful, unique, and mysterious elements of the full course of a human life. Yes, human birth involves suffering, aging, sickness, unhappiness, and ultimately death. But within that span of years between birth and death, truly remarkable things can happen, things that are noble and virtuous and sublime. And nothing is more sublime than love. And love involves attachment. And with attachment there can come suffering. And if the attachment is of the clinging kind, that suffering can be a great affliction.

"But not all attachment, and not all love is like this Ananda, and this is a point which I have failed to express. This is a point on which I have misled many. It is possible to love another human being without the wisdom that recognizes the impermanence of all phenomenal reality, including our embodied existence and the relationships that we establish with other embodied beings. This indeed is a type of attachment which, being rooted in ignorance of the impermanence of all compound things, does indeed lead to affliction, to unhappiness, to states of mental suffering. But there is another kind of love, Ananda. There is kind of love that rejoices in the warmth, tenderness, kindness, dearness, and other wonderful qualities that can be found in a being that one loves – be it the romantic love of two lovers, the love between parent and child, the love of friends, or any kind of genuine love. Indeed, Ananda, even the love between a man and animal, as I knew so well in the attachment that I felt for my beloved horse, Kanthaka,[30] whom I so cruelly left behind at the time of my so-called Great Renunciation.

"Oh Ananda, this is a good and virtuous love, a good and virtuous attachment. This is a love which is fully mindful of the transient nature of all compound things. This is a love which is fully mindful of the inexorable process of change, decay, and the inevitability of death. As such, this is a love grounded in right view, grounded in wisdom. And as such, it makes possible attachment and love in a manner that does not produce afflictive attachment and its consequent suffering. In genuine love, Ananda, it is possible to be fully present with the beloved, to fully embrace the wondrous mystery of that other's existence, to marvel at the peculiar but oh so beautiful connection that draws people together in love. It is possible to experience the sublime nature of love, the participation of two beings as one connected entity.

"I have taught that this love and the attachment associated with it is something which must be avoided. I have proclaimed a dharma in which non-attachment from all things, including all sentient beings, is an essential element of the path to enlightenment. This is an error, Ananda, and one that I now know has brought unnecessary unhappiness to many people.

"It is true that, through my meditative solitude, I discovered that there is a profound and unique joy that is found in the isolated bliss of yogic samadhi. And the pursuit of this bliss is a legitimate path to pursue. But I was mistaken, Ananda, in teaching that it is the only path that can be pursued by one who seeks spiritual fulfillment. Indeed, Ananda, I made a grievous error in teaching that the other path – the path of relationships with other sentient beings – is one that must be abandoned. I have erred in teaching that there can be no path to enlightenment that includes relationships of attachments with others.

"In my own life, Ananda, I look back at my secretive departure from my family – my wife, son, father, and many friends and relatives – and recognize that my action on that night when I left our home while they slept was not an act of spiritual courage but rather an act of spiritual confusion. Indeed, it was an act that was not of a spiritual nature at all, for in it I caused great unhappiness to those who loved me dearly. In a sense, it was a selfish act, carried out with an utterly mistaken sense of selflessness. Oh, how I wish I could undo the hurt that I caused them. And oh, how I wish I could undo the hurt which I unnecessarily caused myself, for by thinking that the pursuit of enlightenment could only be pursued in separation from those who were dear to me, I denied myself that most precious of human experiences – the experience of love.

"So hear me now, Ananda, remember this as you have remembered all of the words that I have uttered, and teach this as a corrective to my error: there is attachment that is afflictive, and there is attachment that is meritous. There is attachment

41

rooted in ignorant clinging and denial of impermanence. This is afflictive. And there is attachment rooted in love and the recognition of the preciousness of our finite embodied existence. This is a good attachment, Ananda. This attachment is not afflictive. This attachment is the attachment of love.

"The attachment of love rooted in wisdom is not an easy thing to pursue, Ananda. Such attachment is rooted in the recognition that there will some day be separation from that to which one is attached. This is an attachment that is fully mindful of impermanence. To love someone and to be fully mindful of the impermanence of the loved one, one's own self, and the relationship that exists between, is indeed an experience that has an element of deep sorrow. And yet it is in this peculiar and mysterious combination of sorrow and love that the depths of the human heart are found. It is in this peculiar and mysterious combination of sorrow and love that the road to true enlightenment can be found.

"Consider, Ananda, the man whose love for his beloved wife is one clouded by craving for constant gratification, jealousy over others, a constant clinging, and the resultant unhappiness whenever there is separation, and perhaps worst of all, that subtle, quiet, but infinitely powerful anxiety over the fear of separation from the beloved...a separation that deep in his heart he knows will someday arrive, since despite all efforts to ignore it, the dark, foreboding awareness of our finitude and the inevitable fact of death is always present in our mind. Such a man, Ananda, is indeed afflicted by misery and unhappiness because of this type of attachment and love. Such a love is indeed a barrier rather than a gateway to spiritual enlightenment. And in teaching the dharma of the universality of suffering, I have perhaps freed some men and women from the burden of this afflictive type of love and attachment.

"But as I have said, Ananda, there is another kind of love. Consider the man whose love for his beloved, though it is a powerful, intense, abiding love, is nonetheless a love that fully recognizes and accepts the finitude of our existence. Accepts the finitude of our existence as a fact that cannot be denied. Such a man, Ananda, does not get caught up in craving, anxiety, jealousy, and anger. Such a man, Ananda, can cherish his beloved in such a deep and profound way that, just thinking about it causes me to weep with joy and sadness – joy over the sublime and beautiful nature of such love; sadness over the deep regret that I have unnecessarily denied such an experience not only to myself, not only to my dear wife Yashodara, but what I can hardly bear – to the thousands of followers of my dharma who have left their homes and left their loved ones and led lives according to the Vinaya.[31]

"Such a sacrifice is not necessary, Ananda, and I command you to correct my grievous error! Tell all that the Buddha has not taught the full dharma. Tell all that the Buddha has taught a spiritual path that is a partial one, a path that brings only the limited bliss of isolation, and does so at such a tremendous and unnecessary cost!

"Tell them, Ananda that there is another path, a greater, fuller, more sublime path. Tell them, Ananda, of the spiritual path of love grounded in wisdom. Tell them to love their family, to love their friends, to love the birds in the air and the beasts on the ground. Tell them to rejoice in their love of the blooming lotus, and tell them to rejoice in their love of each precious moment of samsaric existence, each moment of our precious existence in this embodied life in space and time. Tell them to do this, and to do it in wisdom, which is to say, to do it with a full recognition of impermanence, but with faith that there is a reality that is greater than this finite realm – that, Ananda is the fuller spiritual path, and that is the path which I wish I had taught. Correct my error, Ananda. Begin the process of undoing the harm that I have done."

Chapter 6

The Final Teaching: Suffering

"Oh Ananda, after these many years of experiencing the bliss of what I believed to be enlightenment, to now endure such confusion...such a burden is perhaps more than I can bear. For at this moment, I feel such a strange and confusing mixture of contradictory feelings. To finally acknowledge the flaws of my teaching, to openly express my errors, to release those words which so long had been held back by the dam of my mind, oh it is such a wonderful relief to set aside that burden, as a traveler would feel who sets down a heavy weight which he has carried with him on his journey for thousands of miles. In that sense, I feel light, I feel relieved, I feel as though I am a new-born child, cleansed of all wrong-doing.

"And yet, at the same time – and I cannot explain how such contradictory feelings should reside in the same heart at the same time – I also feel dirty, foul, unclean. I feel as if I have released something that in the many years of being stored inside me in a dark recess of my mind, has fermented and congealed into something repulsive. It is something horribly dark, and that darkness has covered my person, turning me into someone that I do not know, turning me into someone that I loathe, turning me into the most despicable person to ever walk this land. Oh, Ananda, I only hope that I can bear this assault on my equanimity so that I can complete this task of communicating to you the full extent of the errors of my teaching, so that you in turn may teach others this true rendition of the dharma. Bear with me, Ananda, as I engage in this final struggle.

"I have taught the truth of duhkha, or suffering. Indeed, in proclaiming the Four Noble Truths, the truth of duhkha was the first.

"As my followers have heard, as a child and young man I was sheltered from all evidence of suffering by my father, who was fearful that I would become unhappy with worldly life and pursue the path of a religious ascetic. Many people are like me in my youth, hiding from themselves the reality of the pervasive nature of duhkha, engaging in endless diversions and distractions to avoid facing the reality of the suffering that surrounds and engulfs every human life. What a wonderful life of pleasure and beauty that was. Everything around me was full of nothing but life, growth, beauty, and all auspicious qualities. Day after day after day, the early years of my life passed by as I floated through this false nirvana of worldly happiness, seemingly without a care in the world. Oh how fortunate I was – and yet, at the same time, oh how unfortunate I was. Until everything changed...

"My followers also know the account of the Four Sightings, in which I secretly left the palace grounds to see the outside world, whereupon, for the first time in my life, I was exposed to another side of human existence. In successive trips outside the palace walls, driven through the streets of the town by my faithful servant, I viewed for the first time in my life those afflictions which to other men and women were known as simply the nature of life: I was exposed to sickness, aging, and death. How shocking, to me who had been sheltered inside the palace walls for so many years. I was bewildered by the revelation of the

45

unhappiness that afflicts humanity in endless ways. And as a result of the spiritual upheaval that engulfed me from that exposure to duhkha, I eventually chose to leave everything behind – my possessions, the beautiful palace grounds, my father, my wife, even my beloved son. Quietly I left the palace grounds one night while they slept and embarked on the pursuit of spiritual enlightenment, a journey which culminated in my Enlightenment beneath the Bodhi tree and the 45 years of teaching and sangha-building that followed.

"And in those years of teaching, above all else, I taught the Four Noble Truths. As the first, most fundamental truth, the truth from which all other wisdom flowed, the stark, disturbing, painful truth that had to be grasped as the first step to enlightenment, was the First Noble Truth: duhkha. Everything else that I taught followed from the primacy of the universal nature of duhkha, unhappiness, pain, and suffering are our lot in life. They cannot be avoided. They are found everywhere – in towns, in the countryside, in the mountains, by the great sea. They are found among all people, regardless of their status: Brahmins and shudras,[32] rich and poor, men and women, young and old.

"This is a harsh truth, Ananda. It is hard to admit that, lurking behind every moment of happiness, ready to spring forward in the midst of youth, health, and beauty, hiding behind each joyous experience, is the presence of duhkha. And thus I taught many to face and accept with equanimity that which their hearts and minds had sought vainly to deny. Just as I was hidden from duhkha by the protective walls of my father's palace and the false world that he created within the palace grounds, so likewise do all people attempt to create their own walls that allow them to deny the reality of duhkha. But the walls created by people are walls created by their minds, through countless strategies of avoidance and distraction in their daily lives.

"Truly, Ananda, the truth of unhappiness and suffering which I taught was based on a valid insight into the nature of the way things are. Duhkha is indeed found wherever we turn. There is the pain and suffering associated with being embodied beings. Throughout our life, even in infancy and childhood, we are subject to the suffering of illness, injury, hunger and thirst. The horrible deformities with which some are born are only a blatant aspect of this universal suffering, for even those who enjoy the good fortune of being born with a healthy human form are subject to the countless varieties of sickness and disease which can affect even the most healthy of bodies, causing a man who has led a life of health and happiness to be transformed, in a moment, to a being writhing in pain and misery. And to those who elude disease, there is the susceptibility to injury, also of countless varieties. Sometimes caused by the deliberate actions of another being, human or animal. Sometimes caused by pure chance. Again, the man or woman who is healthy and strong can be brought to a state of pain and suffering in a moment by a badly timed accident – a falling tree, lightning from a storm, the sting of a venomous insect or snake. Yes, there are endless ways in which our strong and vibrant bodies become prisons of pain and suffering. No matter how many years of hearty bodily existence we enjoy, all can be brought to an end and transformed into misery in an instant. This is simply the nature of form, Ananda.

"And for those fortunate ones who live out their lives free from disease and injury, there is the inevitable consequence of embodiment: death. Indeed, Ananda, the specter of death hovers over all sentient beings like a hungry ghost, such that even during seemingly sunny days of leisure and enjoyment, we are inwardly suffering at the knowledge that we are residing in an embodied form which is destined for extinction.

"But all duhkha does not derive from embodiment. Indeed, in a sense, the most profound suffering, the unhappiness that runs deepest and is most difficult to eradicate, is not that which is caused by elements outside of us, but that which is generated by our mind and heart. We ceaselessly crave for things which we do not have, and create misery for ourselves in wishing for things, people, places, situations, and all manner of things which we do not have. We experience anger, jealousy, greed, hatred, resentment, and countless other afflictive internal states, all generated by our mind, and all creating a constant state of unhappiness. The person who is healthy worries about becoming ill. The person who is wealthy worries about losing his wealth and gets caught up in the envy of the wealth of others, or looks at the apparent happiness of the poor farmer and envies the happiness of his poverty – while that poor farmer envies and resents the wealth of the man of means. When we are lonely, we suffer the pangs of loneliness. But when we find a beloved, we experience jealousy, suspicion, and worry about the loss of their love. We delight in the joys of having children, but we become angry when they misbehave, we experience guilt when they do not develop into the men and women that we had hoped for. We worry about their health and safety. We search for a perfect match so that when they achieve the age of the householder[33] they will have a good spouse, but then we proceed to enter into a labyrinth of petty conflicts and endless resentments against our in-laws. We work hard to gather wealth so that we can care for our family, and then we spend sleepless nights worrying about the harvest, the weather, the price of our goods, and the always present threat of losing our wealth. And as we age, we look forward to our later years when we might lead a more leisurely life and be cared for by our grown children, but with the thought of those later years comes the anxiety of aging, sickness, disease, loss of our senses, and the ultimate end of death.

"Oh, Ananda, what a strange sort of self-torture it is that we put ourselves through in this life. For in every thing wherein we find happiness, there is the root of craving for more and the fear of loss, and as such, in everything that brings happiness, there comes a guest: duhkha.

"This, Ananda, is the first of the Four Noble Truths: the universality of duhkha. Such is what I taught.

"And further, I taught a path of deliverance from this suffering. I taught the cessation of unhappiness through the cessation of craving. For when one cuts off the desire for something more and different, when one settles for the content of the present moment and is freed from the pernicious sense of constantly pursuing something that one is lacking, a deep sense of calm, abiding happiness emerges. This I taught, Ananda, and this is indeed a path to happiness of a sort, a path that diverts one from the pervasiveness of suffering in this world.

"But Ananda, that is not the entire story! That is not a full account of the nature of existence. This is not the comprehensive dharma. When I taught the truth of the universality of suffering, what I taught was true, but only a partial truth: there is another side to our existence, Ananda. And I failed to teach my followers about that other side of life, and how to enter into it and still find the path to enlightenment. And in teaching only a partial truth, I committed such a grievous error, an error for which I am now atoning in my confession to you and in my admonition to you to go forth and bravely teach to others the corrections to the dharma which I am painfully conveying to you this night, the last in which I shall inhabit this form.

"There is indeed suffering, dear Ananda. But there is also happiness. There is beauty. There is joy. There is virtue. There is kindness. There is love. Oh Ananda, there is so much that is beautiful, wondrous and mysterious about this world of samsara in which we live. Much that is conducive to the acquisition of a deep awareness of the Reality that underlies all phenomenal existence, but that which penetrates it as well.

"Indeed, my friend, the Real is not found only in the act of solitary withdrawal of all sensory awareness, as I have taught to my disciples. The Real is found in each and every moment of Being that we encounter in the act of pure mindfulness.

"To be mindful of that which is internal to our self is indeed a path to liberation and fulfillment. But equally so is the path of mindfulness of, penetration into, and appreciation of that which is external to our consciousness. I have taught the former path at the expense of the latter, and this is the error which I now strive to correct. It is true, Ananda, that that which is external to the mind can be a great fetter, a source of covetous grasping and attachment, and as such a great impediment to enlightenment. But the problem, Ananda – and this is a point that I failed to adequately express, indeed, a point on which I was virtually silent – lies not in the nature of that which is external to the mind, but rather in our *attachment to* and *craving for* that which is external to the mind.

"O Ananda, the arhats are indeed masters at maintaining mindfulness of their body, their thoughts, their feelings, and their mental formations. They are masters at maintaining a steady, fixated, penetrating awareness of that which is present in their own consciousness. And by doing this, they are freed from their own self, recognizing the self as nothing more than its constituent parts. This is indeed a beneficial type of mindfulness.

"But it is not the only type of mindfulness, Ananda."

The Blessed One paused for a moment. I sat there in continued awe and fear, still not comprehending the magnitude of the event that was transpiring before me, still occasionally wondering if I was in the middle of a prolonged dream or hallucination. The Buddha was appearing weary, and he slowly reclined into the Lion's Posture. From that position, he slowly extended his left arm toward the ground, and, raising it, held a small green leaf between his thumb and forefinger. The Blessed One raised the leaf up to his face, holding it just in front of his eyes, softly gazing at it. He moved the tiny leaf beneath his nose and gently inhaled. He placed the edge of the leaf in his mouth, moistened his lips, and appeared to actually taste the delicate green leaf. And then, holding the stem of the leaf in one hand, with the index of his finger of the other hand he slowly stroked the leaf, so gently and softly, as if he was traversing huge mountain ranges as his finger moved along the ridges of the veins of the leaf with such profound subtlety.

"Ah!...Ah!... How wonderful. How brilliant. How sublime. Oh Ananda, to be mindful of this tiny piece of reality which we designate with the word 'leaf'...oh, such a miraculous experience! Its color – that which we designate by the word 'green'. How beautiful. Indeed, how remarkable that we experience color at all. Light, color, shade. A thousand shades of grey as seen in a cloudy sky of an approaching storm. The endless greens that strike our eyes when we gaze upon the forest. The deep blue of the seas and lakes and streams, mingling with light and flecks of green and black and grey and countless other shades as the water passes through the ripples. Oh Ananda, this dear, dear leaf, in all its wonder, trailing clouds of glory in its simple beauty.

"To be mindful of this leaf, and to be mindful of nothing else, and to be penetratingly mindful of it in all of its depth and grandeur. Oh, Ananda, my spirit could explode at a moment like this. Oh Ananda, the precious fullness of being, found in the quiet, subtle, humble simplicity of this dear leaf. Of this wonder, what can be said?

"Ananda, that is what I have failed to teach. Great shame I have earned, many years in hellish regions of torment I deserve. For in leading men and women down one path, I have hidden the other path from them: the path of joy in deep mindfulness of the depth of being. Oh, Ananda, please forgive me for this, and please correct the wrong that I have done. The color. The scent. The taste. The touch. Indeed, Ananda, I can even hear the subtle vibratory sound emanating from this tiny piece of being. All of this is so wonderful and precious that my heart could explode.

"I have taught the Four Foundations of Mindfulness, in which I have instructed the meditator to be mindful of the body and its sensations; the mind and its thoughts; the heart and its feelings; and the various mental formations that clog up our consciousness. All of this is very useful to a point, and conducive to a certain type of peaceful healing to one who has been afflicted with a mind and heart that is scattered, drawn in a thousand directions by the various temptations that arise from grasping and wrong view. It does bring about freedom from the monkey mind[34] and the establishment of a state of quiescence[35].

"But what about mindfulness of a leaf! This too leads to a purified mind. This too is the path to bliss. Indeed, in the mindful perception of this leaf, the path to nirvana is found.

"Ananda, how many seasons have we spent in the mango grove,[36] surrounded by the orchards of full fruit? Here, my friend, is a mango that has been brought to me as a gift. How many times have I accepted such fruit with gratitude, only to set it aside, seeing it only as a temptation to give in to the sensuality of taste, and hence disrupt my meditative equanimity? And have I not taught my followers to guard against not only the cravings of taste, but to guard all of the portals of the senses, teaching that access to the enlightened mind and release from suffering can only come from detachment from all sensual pleasures? And yet now, Ananda, I taste this mango. Ah! What sweetness. The soft, delicate texture is such a joy to my mouth. How it nourishes the body. How its life intermingles with that of my own body as it descends into my stomach. In the simple joy of mindfully tasting this humble piece of fruit, there is the fullness of the wisdom of enlightenment, just as there is in the mindful vision of the beauty of the leaf. There is no need to fear the mango, or the leaf, or any aspect of the sensory world, as long as it is experienced with right view. And what is right view? Right view is the recognition of the transient, impermanent nature of all phenomenal reality. And from this right view comes the freedom from attachment and craving. This is a delicate and subtle step for the mind to take, Ananda, and out of fear of not adequately conveying this to others, I instead taught the easy path of renunciation of the phenomenal world. But renunciation is not necessary when one holds to right view. Indeed, once one has become firmly established in the understanding of things as they really are, then and only then one can deeply penetrate the wonder of being, the mysterious and miraculous nature of perception and experience of the beauty of this world. To achieve this penetrating experience of the world and simultaneously recognize its frail transience, and consequently to avoid falling into the error of craving is indeed a task far more difficult than even the most severe asceticism. To allow one's awareness to fully penetrate that which is perceived, to appreciate it fully in its momentary existence, to be fully present with the world for but a moment – this, Ananda, leads to a blissful experience that far exceeds that which is attained in the path of renunciation that I have taught.

"I have taught the Four Foundations of Mindfulness,[37] in which I have instructed the meditator to be mindful of the body and its sensations; the mind and its thoughts; the heart and its feelings; and the various mental formations that clog up our consciousness. All of this is very useful to a point, and conducive to a certain type of peaceful healing to one who has been afflicted with a mind and heart that is scattered, drawn in a thousand directions by the various temptations that arise from grasping and wrong view.

"But what about mindfulness of the taste of a mango! This too leads to a purified mind. This too is the path to bliss. Indeed, in the mindful perception of this fruit, the path to nirvana is found.

"Ananda, my dear friend, my sole confessor, the one who will dispel the errors that I have taught and reveal to the Sangha, monks and laypersons alike, the true dharma in the fullness of its mysterious and ineffable beauty – Oh Ananda, have you never sat quietly at twilight time, at the magical moment when the day has yielded to the night but the night has not yet accepted its role. The wonderful moment of the in-between, that liminal moment, when neither day nor night are unambiguously ascendant, that moment when both day and night are present in the waning and waxing modes of their being. What a wonderful moment that is, and what a delicious experience – yes, Ananda, I did indeed use the word delicious, for I draw in each moment of that experience, I consume it, I devour it, I swim in the nectar of bliss that such a moment of the conjunction of day and night bring forth. Especially, Ananda, on a clear evening, when the line across the horizon is a clear one, as if a line of deep blue indigo ink has been drawn across the sky. And above that line, oh such subtle shades of orange, red, blue, grey – colors so subtle that only a mindful eye can see them. Yet colors that, to that mindful eye, are radiant in their exquisitely subtle expression.

"And as it sometimes happens, on a moment so precious and rare, at that very moment of dusk when the day and night are melting together, there arises the evening breeze. Oh, Ananda, I can feel that subtle coolness on my skin. I can smell the subtle fragrance carried on the breeze. A breeze that calms the heart and mind, a breeze that seems to say, "Let us now put the day to rest, and bring on the peaceful sleep of the night, as it has always been and as it shall always be." Oh, such a wonderful, blissful, ineffable moment. And this, too, Ananda, is a moment of mindfulness that can lead to enlightenment. This too is a moment of mindfulness of the beauty and fullness of being that leads to the same wisdom as that acquired by the path of renunciation and internal retreat that I have taught. Such pity do I feel for those who, because of my teaching, have felt it necessary to deny themselves these beauties of the world, those prescient, sublime moments of the relationship of mind to being.

"And it is true, the moment of twilight lasts for but a few minutes, and it passes on to the black of night. The enlightening cool breeze blows but for a few moments, and then it is gone, overtaken by the stillness of the night. Yes, Ananda, like all things, the cool breeze is transient. And yet, like all transient things, it too can be a source of wisdom, a source of enlightenment. Attachment to the breeze, grasping at the breeze, yearning for the breeze to remain for more than its allotted time – all these are approaches that are misguided and not conducive to enlightenment. But the flaw is not in the breeze or in the experience of the breeze – the flaw is in the mind of the one who perceives the breeze. I can grasp at the breeze and falsely hope that that brief profound moment might last forever, all of which leads to suffering; or I can accept the breeze for what it is, a transitory expression of the fullness of being, and deeply penetrate its nature through sublime mindfulness, and as such ride the vehicle of the transitory breeze to the fullness of enlightenment.

"I have taught the Four Foundations of Mindfulness, in which I have instructed the meditator to be mindful of the body and its sensations; the mind and its thoughts; the heart and its feelings; and the various mental formations that clog up our consciousness. All of this is very useful to a point, and conducive to a certain type of peaceful healing to one who has been afflicted with a mind and heart that is scattered, drawn in a thousand directions by the various temptations that arise from grasping and wrong view.

"But what about mindfulness of the breeze at dusk? This too leads to a purified mind. This too is the path to bliss. Indeed, in the mindful perception of this breeze, the path to nirvana is found.

"Of course, Ananda, it is true that every aspect of phenomenal reality – everything about the world in which we live – is subject to change, decay, and extinction. And hence, for one who becomes attached, phenomenal reality can be a source of suffering. And the gentle serene wind that so deeply stirs the spirit can be replaced by the terrifying gales of the storm. In times of famine, flood, and storm, the leaf withers, and the sweet fruit rots, the wind destroys. And the realm of nature, which at times can be a source of such beauty and inspiration, can become a cruel carrier of the most heartless array of endless varieties of pain, torment, disease, and grief. The child who starves, the old mother who grieves at the death of her child, the farmer whose crops are destroyed, and the family whose dwelling is swept away – all of this suffering does indeed derive from the phenomena of nature, the very phenomena that I have just taught can be a source of enlightenment.

"But therein lays the paradox of life, Ananda, a paradox which I fear I have failed to give adequate heed to during my ministry. It is true that all things can lead to duhkha. But it is also true those very same things can lead to the supreme happiness. And the wise one is he who is mindful of this paradox at all times: mindful of the potential to produce suffering, the wise one refrains from craving, attachment, and clinging; but mindful of the potential to bring joy, the wise one mindfully embraces the full nature of being, precious and brilliant even in its transient nature. The leaf, the fruit, the breeze – all may be guides to the experience of the profound nature of reality, and as such all are teachers of liberation. So it is not necessary to renounce experience of the world of phenomena; indeed it is not necessary to renounce enjoyment of the world of phenomena, as I have previously taught. It is not necessary to close the portals of the senses and embark on the path of the monk, as I have I taught to so many over these past years. Such a path is permissible, and such a path can lead to inner tranquility and enlightened wisdom.[38] But this is not the only path, and it is here that I have erred and misled so many. The path of experiencing being, experiencing it in the depths of profound mindfulness, experiencing it in full awareness of the transient nature of all phenomena – this too is a path to the highest bliss, this too is a path to enlightenment. For those who choose to renounce the world and seek enlightenment, let them do so, and may they find that which they seek. But for those who wish to embrace the world in mindfulness of its true nature, so let them follow that path as well, and they too will find what they seek.

Chapter 7

The Final Teaching: The Self

Once again the Blessed One paused, and with that pause the enormity of the situation descended upon me with full force. Perhaps I had been so caught up in hearing every shocking word that the Buddha uttered that I had not fully recognized the significance of those words. Only now, in the profound and powerful silence of the pause in this, his final teaching, did I realize that I was hearing a teaching that could radically change the Sangha. In a sense, I could not believe what I was hearing – the all-wise, enlightened Buddha declaring that he had been in error and repudiating his own teachings – teachings that he had delivered over the span of four decades to tens of thousands of devotees. Such sorrow and such compassion I felt for the Blessed One, for surely this was the darkest moment of his life. Or perhaps not – perhaps this was the supreme relief, the cleansing that would free him to truly enter into his final nirvana and forever escape return to the troubled realm of samsara. But what a burden it must have been to carry those doubts within him for all those years, and with no one to share them with, no one to confide in. Perhaps I myself had been amiss at not presenting myself to the Buddha as one to whom he could speak about anything. And yet, how presumptuous it would have been for me, a devoted but lowly monk, to have thought that the Blessed One would have entered into such a conversation with me or any of the other devotees. He was seen as a supremely enlightened being, the source of pure, liberating wisdom. Surely he knew that any expression of doubt on his part about the very words that he taught would have been devastating to those who looked to him as their guide to liberation, and surely he felt a duty to meet their expectations of him as the teacher of the flawless path to nirvana. And hence, with those seeds of doubt brewing within for many years, and with utterly no one to share those doubts with in hope of dispelling them, what an agonizing existence he must have experienced behind that appearance of blissful composure and equanimity. How deeply sorrowful I felt for this, my teacher and friend, and as we sat there in the silence of his pause, I quietly wept.

And yet, I also was beginning to recognize that there was a sense to what he was saying. The subtle truth which he was communicating on this, his final night, was indeed starting to fit together. While part of me wanted to shout, "Master, stop it!" in order to release him from such pain, another part of me was slowly realizing that the words that he spoke were indeed wise and sublime, and my compassionate wish for him to stop fought with my desire to hear more.

But it was not just the Buddha's welfare that I worried about. I also contemplated the enormous burden that I would be left with if the Buddha expected me to convey this teaching to his followers. Would they believe me? Would they ever believe that the Buddha had issued a repudiation of his teachings, and that he had done so during the final hours of his earthly life, and delivered these teachings in private, to none but me? Surely not! How could they be expected to believe what I was hearing on this dreadful night? And why would they believe me, of all people? My position within the Sangha, despite my many years of devoted service to the Blessed One, was already somewhat controversial.[39] Lacking a witness, surely I would be labeled as a liar or a deluded madman, or perhaps I would be accused of trying to take over the Sangha as the monk Devadatta had done earlier in the Buddha's ministry. In any case, I was sure to be reviled by my fellow monks.

Indeed, despite my renown as one who could memorize and recite every word that I heard, I now began to doubt my own ability. In light of the shattering nature of the night's experience, would I still be able to accurately recall each of the Buddha's words during this, his final sutra? Could I trust my own memory, especially when it was hearing words that caused so much pain to my Master, and hence were words which I wished had never been spoken?

These and many more profound matters I pondered as the now silent Buddha sat in front of me, once again looking old, weary, and deflated.

And yet, once again before my eyes, I saw the life return to him, I saw his features assume that quality of subtle, composed strength, that was always present during his sermons. Slowly the slumped form assumed a straightened posture, the equanimity returned to his face, and a sense of confidence and certitude once more radiated from the Master. And from this position which I had come to know so well over the decades, the Blessed One resumed his teaching.

"So it is seen, my friend, that the obstacle to wisdom and the barrier to nirvana is not the world itself, but rather the attitude that we adopt toward that world. There is mind, and there are those things that are perceived as external to the mind; and those things perceived as external to the mind we come to designate as the 'world', even though such a dualistic designation is not entirely accurate.[40] It is not the world, but the nature of our belief about that world, that impedes our spiritual progress. It is not the world, but the wrong belief that the elements of that world will always be there. It is the failure to recognize the universal nature of the impermanence of all things.

"And from this erroneous view of the world as consisting of entities that endure, we form attachments – attachments that lead to suffering, for that to which we become attached is destined to decay, to dissipate, to disappear and cease to exist. But the attachment itself is not the problem, Ananda. Attachment is accompanied by fondness for the object or experience of attachment. Fondness, Ananda, is not in itself harmful. Indeed, I should say that fondness is a wonderful quality of experience, as long as it is rooted in wisdom.

"There are two types of attachment, Ananda. There is attachment rooted in ignorance, and attachment rooted in wisdom. Attachment and fondness rooted in ignorance is that which fails to recognize the inevitable impermanence of the object of attachment. This type of attachment causes only grief and suffering, Ananda.

"But there is also attachment and fondness rooted in wisdom. This is attachment and fondness which, while recognizing the miraculous, wondrous nature of the object, simultaneously recognizes the impermanence of the object and the impermanent nature of the experience of happiness, joy, or pleasure that is derived from the object. Such attachment rooted in the wisdom of impermanence is not an obstruction to the path to enlightenment. To the contrary, when pursued with constant, profound, sublime mindfulness, it can be the path to the most supreme, blissful, incomparable fulfillment.

"One need not flee the world to obtain the supreme spiritual path, Ananda. This is what I have taught, but it is only a half-truth, and it is what I shall correct this very night. One can indeed find liberation through the path of withdrawal from the world, but far superior to that is the path of one who immerses himself in the profound depths of the world, experiencing all of its joys and sorrows, letting the world penetrate one's being to the very marrow – but doing so in full mindfulness of the universality of impermanence, and hence doing so free from harmful attachment. Such a seeker walks the tightrope, the exquisitely fine line between fleeing from the world and becoming afflictively attached to the world. Such a person can see a leaf, taste a fruit, feel an evening breeze – such a person can soak in the fullness of conscious experience of the wondrous world – and do so without afflictive attachment.

"Such a path of detached immersion in the world is exceedingly difficult, Ananda. It is difficult to experience the leaf, the fruit, the breeze in such a manner. But the truly difficult task, the task which few can accomplish, the task which perhaps I myself have failed at, is the task of which I shall now speak. Hear me carefully, O friend.

"To understand the true nature of the leaf, the fruit, and the breeze, and to relate to each in a spiritual manner is one thing. But to relate to another self: to another person, to a wife, a son or daughter, a dear friend, a stranger passing in the road, a great ruler, a lowly servant. To relate to a self, and to truly understand the nature of the self, and to experience that self in an enlightened manner – truly, Ananda, that is the greatest challenge for those who pursue the path to liberation.

"And what have I taught about the self, Ananda? Surely you recall that I have compared the self to a wheel. That which we refer to by the word 'wheel,' is composed of various parts: an axle, spokes, and a rim. What are we left with when we discard the axle, spokes, and rim. Where then is the 'wheel?'"

I replied, "As you have often said, master, once the parts are removed, it is clear that there is no wheel. And indeed, there never was such an object as a 'wheel' with an independent existence. Rather, 'wheel' is simply a word, a designation, a concept which we create with the mind to conveniently refer to a particular combination of axle, spokes, and rim. Once the parts are gone, the non-existence of the 'wheel' is revealed."

"Excellent, Ananda. You have learned well the words which I have taught over these many years. Just as it is with the wheel, so I have I taught it is with the self. I have taught the doctrine of *anatman*, or no-self. What we call the 'self' is composed of the Five Aggregates. There is the form, or body; there are thoughts; there are feelings; there are the various mental formations and perceptions; and there is consciousness in general. But once we remove these aggregates, where then is the self? It is nowhere to be seen. As I have taught, what we commonly refer to as 'self' is merely a word, a designation, a concept which we create in order to conveniently refer to a particular combination of the Five Aggregates. Once the aggregates are gone, the non-existence of an independent 'self' is revealed.

"What are the consequences of such a teaching, Ananda? I have taught that, as a result of the constructed, illusory nature of the self, the self is something that one should abandon. I have taught that this applies to one's own self, by abandoning the 'needs' that the worldly person believes are generated by the falsely constructed self, and I have taught that one should abandon other selves and pursue the life of the monk, detached from all human relationships other than those which are necessary to maintain the successful functioning of the Sangha. I have encouraged followers to abandon home, wife, family, kin, friends, neighbors. What I have taught, Ananda, truly encourages followers to perceive the path to enlightenment as a path involving progressive detachment from the selves that clog up our life.

"In the teaching to the sannyasin Kandaraka,[41] I taught that nothing, not even another person, is worth becoming attached to. Thus I declared, 'Household life is cloudy and dusty; life gone forth is wide open. It is not easy, while living in a home, to lead the holy life utterly perfect and pure as a polished shell...put on the yellow robe, and go forth from the home life into homelessness.'[42] And such a going forth into the homeless life means leaving behind one's wife, children, family and friends, as I myself once did on the night of my Great Renunciation.

"Indeed, Ananda, I have spoken bluntly to those who suffer from the loss of a loved one, such as the householder who approached me in the Jeta Grove in Anathapindika's Park, grieving over the loss of his beloved son. To this man I stated, 'So it is householder, so it is! Sorrow, lamentation, pain, grief, and despair are born from those who are dear; arise from those who are dear.'[43] This is what I taught, Ananda, that only unhappiness and suffering come from attachment to those who are dear.

"And so many men, and even a few women,[44] have left their homes, their spouses and their children, their parents and friends, and embarked on the life of the monk who seeks only nirvana, free from any attachments to others, free from the clinging to those who are dear to one. And this path is a path that is appropriate for some. The path of detachment from the world is, in fact, the easy path, for it is a path which sidesteps the challenge of achieving, implementing, and retaining one's enlightened mindfulness even in the midst of the glories and the tragedies of the world.

"Recall, Ananda, that this is the path that I myself have followed, known as the Great Renunciation. Even though I had a devoted father, a beautiful and loving wife, and a sweet young son, I snuck away from them in the middle of the night to embark upon the path of a sannyasin, thinking that such a homeless life was necessary to achieve spiritual enlightenment.

"And looking back, I now grieve over the many, many people for whom my teachings have caused unnecessary grief. I have harmed many, Ananda, and it was a harm that did not have to happen. I have caused much grief to my followers, and I have caused much grief to the families and friends that they have left behind to follow me. How many wives were left grieving for the lost embrace of their husband, left alone in an empty house, sleeping in an empty bed? How many children cried and wondered why their father, who had hugged them, played with them, told them stories, and displayed all the wonderful things that only a father can for his child, had disappeared, had abandoned them, never to return? How many aging parents were left to fend for themselves when their once devoted and loyal son left the home and all of its responsibilities to seek the spiritual path?

"And all of this was unnecessary, Ananda! I chose to teach only the easy path, the path of detachment from the world. The path rooted in the teaching of no-self. And hearing this teaching, of course those who longed for nirvana chose to leave home, for that indeed was the only way to follow that path.

"But that is not the only path! There is another path, Ananda, a path whose dimensions are exceedingly subtle and virtually impossible to describe. A path about which one who has found it is tempted to say nothing at all, since the accurate description of this path through the imperfect medium of human language can so easily lead to error. It is a path that is difficult to teach, and difficult to follow, but it is a path that does not require renunciation of all that one holds dear. It is a path that does not cause grief and misery to the loved ones who embark on the path. It is a path that allows one to see the leaf, to taste the fruit, to enjoy the breeze, and to love one's wife, child, parent, friend – to love any and all who cross one's path.

"And this path, which I have been teaching you this night, Ananda, is a path rooted in a view of the self that is deeper than the view which I have previously taught the Sangha. I have not misled my beloved monks, but I have not communicated to them the fullness of the nature of the self. Perhaps you recall that on several occasions, I was asked by an arhant to speak on the nature of the self, and on each occasion I avoided a direct answer to the question.[45] I did so because of the subtle nature of a true understanding of the self, and out of fear that my teaching would be misunderstood and lead the monks away from the path to enlightenment on which they had embarked. Looking back, I regret that decision – oh how I wish I had summoned the courage to articulate a fuller view of the self and the nature of the path that does not require the renunciation of the homeless one. Oh how much less grief I would have caused! So hear me now, Ananda, as I teach my final teaching: the teaching on the nature of the self and the path of non-renunciation.

"There is a self, and then there is a different Self.

"There is the self that I have taught as the assemblage of the five aggregates. And then there is a different Self.

"There is the self that ceases to exist once the aggregates are gone, the self that is nowhere to be found once body, thought, feeling, mental content, and individual consciousness are gone. And then there is a different Self.

"There is the self which we identify with as an entity that is labeled 'I'. And then there is a different Self.

"There is the self that is identified by a name and form, and assumed to be connected with a specific body. And then there is a different Self.

"There is the self which engages in an endless variety of daily affairs, perceiving itself as the actor in these affairs, perceiving itself as a real and permanent entity interacting with the world, exhausting its energy in an effort to build for itself a position of wealth, reputation, and success in this world. And then there is another Self.

"There is the self which clings and craves and forms selfish, afflictive attachments to people, things, experiences, places, ideas, memories, and all sorts of objects of attachment. And then there is a different Self.

"There is a self which is the product of karmic influences and causes and conditions, plummeting through life tossed from one unhappy state to another, always subject to the laws of causation while naively believing in its own autonomy. And then there is a different Self.

"There is a self which is impermanent but craves for immortality, and consequently lives each and every moment with the burden of denying its own inevitable death and lives each and every moment with the gnawing anxiety that its deluded denial of death might be a fiction, and that annihilation is indeed its unavoidable destiny. And then there is a different Self.

"There is the self whose false sense of ego-identification and consequent deluded attachments leads to unhappiness and grief. And then there is a different Self.

"Ananda, think of the mother who lovingly holds and gazes upon her infant son. Imagine her, as a typical mother, delighting in the little one's cooing and laughing, its smile, its sweet and innocent gestures. Does the mother gaze into her son's eyes and think: 'Dearest child, if only you knew what you truly are. You are nothing but a heap of aggregates, a temporary formation of form and mind, a combination of bodily and mental factors. And behind that, there is – nothing! Yes, my little one, there is the reality of anatman. You are nothing but the temporary product of multiple impersonal karmic forces that have brought together this collection of components that hang together for a short period of time, during which you are given a name, a name which deludes you and others into thinking that there is something more substantial and abiding about your self than a mere collection of elements. Dearest child, you are nothing more than that. And because you are nothing more than that, and because I have been blessed with knowledge of the dharma which teaches the truth of no-self and the necessity of non-attachment, I shall not become attached to you, I shall not love you, I shall not long for you when we are apart, I shall not worry for you in times of peril, and above all, I shall not grieve for you in death.'

"Tell me Ananda, what would you think of a mother so thoroughly grounded in the dharma?"

The Blessed One had brought me to a state of confusion. The

logic of his words led me to recognize that the mother's thoughts were true to the Buddha's dharma, and yet my heart – like the heart of any man or woman with the capacity for kindness and compassion – found the mother's words to be revolting, hideous, unspeakably cruel. And thus I said to the Blessed One,

"Your words confuse me, Master. For the mother's thoughts seem to be in full accord with the dharma that you have taught, and yet I find those thoughts to be revolting and evil, as I believe would any person with a heart. Please help me, Blessed One, please clarify the confusion that your words have created in your servant's befuddled mind!" But instead of answering my plea, in keeping with his fondness for repetition,[46] the Buddha presented another example.

"Picture, Ananda, a man of many years whose beloved wife has died. Theirs has been a good marriage, characterized by kindness, tender feelings, many children, and the deep happiness that sometimes can come from a long life lived together. Yet his neighbors are puzzled at the absence of grief displayed by the widower. His friends cannot understand the calm demeanor and attitude of disinterest in the death of his wife that he displays. At the time of his wife's cremation, he calmly approaches the funeral pyre and lights it without the slightest hesitation or visible sign of emotion. His closest friend of many decades, after observing this peculiar reaction, approaches him as the flames rise higher and higher, and says, 'O friend, I do not understand the lack of grief and the sense of indifference that you display as your beloved wife is consumed by the flames, never again to be embraced in your arms.'

"And to this the widower calmly replies to his friend: 'What I have lost is merely a bundle of aggregates. What burns in the fire is merely a bag of bones. I have lived many years with that which, like all compound things, was in a state of constant change and destined to extinction. What should I grieve over, for there was never anything of substance there to begin with...only the temporary collection of name and form that we mistakenly call a self.'

"And what, Ananda, would you think of this widower, who clearly was a student of the dharma taught from my lips?"

Once again, as before, the Master had brought me to a state of great confusion. Viewing the widower from the perspective of the human heart, his words repulsed me. And yet, viewing his words from the perspective of the dharma, I had to acknowledge that indeed they seemed to be in accord with the teachings of the Blessed One. So once again, I implored the Buddha to relieve me of this burden of confusion and clear up my befuddled mind.

"Yes, Ananda, there is a Self that is more than just the combination of name, form, and mental dispositions which we superficially identify as 'me.'

"There is, indeed, Ananda, something that is deeper and more abiding than that superficial self. There is indeed that elusive something that the loving mother sees in a child – not just the child's body, its name, its observable traits – but something much deeper than that, and it is that deeper Self that elicits the love of the mother for the child. And there is something in the wife that is no longer present in her deceased body which causes her husband to weep at having lost something rare, precious, and unique. It is not her name, form, or mental dispositions that he misses and grieves for, but something that transcends all of these transient components of the superficial self. When Yama arrives as the bringer of death, we sense that something leaves. More than just the loss of vitality in the body, something essential leaves at death – that, Ananda, is the true Self, the Self that leads parents to grieve over lost children and lovers to experience bliss in the embrace of their beloved.

"This true Self – how obvious it is to even the most simple-minded, and yet how elusive it is when we try to define it! How easy it is to sense this true Self, yet how hard it is to resist the temptation to confuse it with the transient superficial self and become attached to the wrong thing. Even now, Ananda, my weariness returns when I think of the difficulty that I would experience in trying to explain the true Self to you, and how it differs from, but is intimately entangled with, the superficial self during our lives on this Earth.

"When we perceive another person, especially a person that we love, what exactly do we perceive, Ananda? Certainly we do indeed perceive those transient temporal elements which someday will be dissolved when death arrives. But do we not also perceive something else, something that has a rare, precious, indefinable quality, something that leads us to treat that other person in a special way, different from the way in which we might treat a rock or a block of wood? Why do we treat our loved ones different from a rock or block of wood? Because we recognize that there is something unique in our loved one, something that is not present in the rock or block of wood, no matter how beautiful in their own way they might be. Yes, Ananda, we recognize that in another person whom we love we have sensed something that is marvelous, transcendent, miraculous. It is hard to define, but it is there – and that is the true Self.

"We see the miracle of consciousness existing in an embodied human form. How wondrous! How inexpressible! That something of the nature of mind should somehow be entangled with something of the nature of form. How mysterious that the free and infinite mind should come to dwell in a fixed point in time and space – to dwell as this specific, unique entity known as a person. And how wonderful that the consciousness that is my own should be able to identify and communicate with the consciousness of another. And how astounding that we can sense that there is something utterly unique and precious about each of those Selves that we encounter, recognizing that the skandha-composed body shall indeed reach an end and disintegrate when death arrives, but the Self, the mind, the consciousness shall not perish. We recognize that the conscious being, the person, that we perceive is indeed an utterly unique entity, existing at this particular point in space and time in a manner that differentiates itself from all other conscious beings existing at this point in space and time and all beings existing at other points in space and time. Yes, Ananda, every person that we meet is an utterly unique being. And to befriend that person, to love that person, is to fully embrace the precious nature of that unique being and unique event – just that combination of mind and matter at just that moment in space and time. Oh, how marvelous, how miraculous, how rare, how mysterious![47]

"And exactly what is it that makes each person unique, what is it that constitutes this true 'Self' behind the superficial, transient self? I really cannot articulate that, Ananda. On that I must remain silent. And yet, despite my silence, I would affirm that the sense of the preciousness and uniqueness of each person is so immediately apparent to anyone who has opened his heart that it requires no explanation. One does not need an explanation to know the wetness of water. One just knows it. One just experiences it, in an immediate awareness. And so it is with the true Self.

"This is not to deny, Ananda, that the particular constellation of body and mind which constitutes a person will inevitably cease to exist as an integrated unit upon death. I have taught that all compound things are transient, and the person, as a compound of name and form, body and spirit, is indeed a transient entity which will face death and dissolve as a compound entity. Like all things, it is subject to the law of impermanence. But its transient nature does not negate its value. In fact, its transient nature makes it all the more precious, for knowing that this miraculous entity – this combination of body and mind, this person – will someday cease to exist in its form as that person, makes it all the more precious.

"The wise one, Ananda, recognizes this preciousness, appreciates this preciousness, embraces this preciousness. And because of the appreciation of this preciousness, there arises in the wise one a sense of infinite compassion, kindness, and love for this being.

"And what is it, Ananda, which makes a person so precious? Is there not something present in the person that exists in addition to the five aggregates? Is there not something, elusive and subtle, that is present in the person which continues to exist in some manner even after the dissolution of the aggregates? What that is, is hard to define, Ananda, and indeed, I shall not even attempt to do so. But it can be known, it can be sensed, it can be experienced by anyone – anyone who loves another, anyone who grieves for a friend lost to death, anyone who experiences the joy of the parent who brings a new child into the world. What we sense at such moments is the true Self that transcends the superficial self. What we sense at these moments is the Self that exists independent of the self which is dependent on and composed of the aggregates.

"I have taught the doctrine of no-self, Ananda, but indeed I did not teach it with sufficient accuracy, clarity, and rigor. For if my words had been more carefully chosen, I would have distinguished between the transient self that is composed of the impermanent aggregates and dissolves upon death, and the true Self which transcends all. I taught non-attachment to the concept of self, and that is indeed a wise teaching, but I should have taught non-attachment to the impermanent self only. To be attached to the impermanent self and to crave for its permanency is indeed a source of unhappiness and a barrier on the road to enlightenment. But to long for, to love, to yearn for the wondrous beauty of the true Self, all the while recognizing the transient nature of the shell in which it resides – there is nothing to be rejected in this, Ananda, and indeed, this is a path to true awakening, when we recognize the distinction between what is transient and what is abiding, even while it appears in the shell of the transient.

"Had I recognized this, I would not have left my wife, I would not have left my dear young son, I would not have left my aging father. And I would not have set forth a teaching which has now led countless others to bring pain and heartache into their homes as they too, following my words, believed that such relationships of dearness must be cast aside to pursue the spiritual path. But tonight, Ananda, through what I declare unto you, I correct the errors that I have made and ask you to share this teaching with those who have looked to me for wisdom and guidance.

"I can see, my good friend, that you are pondering the obvious question: why did I teach in error in the first place? Why did I offer a teaching that was flawed?

"Truly, even now as I feel the life ebb from my body, I cannot say with certainty why I have made this grievous mistake. Indeed, Ananda, in a sense I did not so much make a mistake in presenting a false teaching as I failed to communicate the entire truth and present the dharma in its full form. What I have previously taught as the dharma – the way of detachment, the way of isolation, the way of setting aside one's awareness of the world of senses for the sake of an awareness of the spacious beauty of our consciousness, of mind alone – that is indeed a valid path to a state of spiritual bliss. It does indeed bring profound peace and tranquility. It is indeed a true dharma which brings release from the sufferings of samsaric existence. And in this sense, to the extent that many have followed this path which I have taught, I have indeed brought happiness to many who would otherwise be immersed in lives of pain, unhappiness, and suffering.

"That was a valid path, but it was not the only path, for as I have taught you this very night, the full awareness of the precious and sublime nature of the realm of time and space is also a path to liberation, as long as one's awareness of the fullness of time and space is recognized as an impermanent realm to which one must not become attached. And why did I not teach this path before? I cannot say, Ananda. And my mind ...my mind is weary, and it no longer wishes to engage in the strenuous task of pointless analysis and explanation. Why did I not teach this path before? Perhaps because it is only this very night that I have fully understood it! Perhaps – as I think back in retrospect on those many years of my teaching – I always sensed that there was another path, but I was afraid to admit it, afraid to even allow myself to think about the possibility that the dharma as I had delivered it to thousands upon thousands of suffering men and women, was not the only dharma. Perhaps it is only tonight, with the knowledge of the rapid approach of my own death, that my mind had been released from its selfish protection of the dharma that has gained me great renown, freed to finally acknowledge the worm that that had been quietly but incessantly gnawing away at my spirit for these past forty-some years, freed to finally concede that there is another path, a path that embraces rather than withdraws from the smell of the flower, the taste of the fruit, the embrace of the lover.

"Of course, Ananda, one question remains: If there is indeed some sort of Self that persists, some sort of Self that is precious and good, some sort of Self that is more real than the superficial self that we identify with our transient name and form, what happens to that Self after death?

"This is a profound and subtle matter, one which I am reluctant to say much about, for once again we are touching on an issue which words are inadequate to express, an issue which cannot be communicated in clear and comprehensive terms through the limiting medium of the use of sound fashioned into the paltry, limiting structures of that which we call the human word. We are dealing here with yet another matter that is perhaps best left as a mystery, and yet I know that the hunger of the human mind to gain understanding from the concepts generated by that mind – that is to say, through words – cannot be easily set aside, and hence I shall offer a response to that question, feeble and inadequate as those words might be.

"Remember, Ananda, how I was previously asked by my

disciples about the ultimate destiny of the self? And how did I respond at that time?"

"Your response, my Lord, was a response that I truly could not comprehend. Your words left me dizzy. For you declared that it is neither the case that after death of the body the self exists, nor that the self does not exist, nor that the self neither exists nor does not exist, nor that the self both exists and does not exist."[48]

"Indeed, Ananda, such was my response. In a sense it was a true response, and yet in another sense it was perhaps a very inadequate and misleading response. For while my words were, in a sense, quite true, they were true only in the sense that the truth about the ultimate nature of the Self is a truth that transcends our capacity to articulate the ultimate nature of things through the use of words and constructions of rational argument. Perhaps if I had remained silent, my response would have been equally valid and instructive.

"Describing the true nature of the Self once it has been freed from its connection to the transient body and the aggregates is a task that requires a delicacy of expression and subtlety of thought that is virtually impossible to achieve and maintain. It is like walking on the narrowest of tightropes, where the slightest loss of balance leads to a calamitous plunge into error on either the side of affirming a falsely existent self or the equally egregious error of denying the existence of the true Self. Even now, especially now, as I feel my strength wane and the vital energies gathering in my heart for the final ascent and exit from my soon-to-be lifeless body, I fear that I am not up to the task.

"Nonetheless, in the hope that I might at least begin the process of rectifying the errors that I have made in my earlier teaching of the dharma, let me attempt with my diminishing strength to utter a few brief words on this matter that, in truth, cannot be adequately conveyed through the medium of language."

I waited in eager anticipation of the Blessed One's words of wisdom, prepared to listen to each word, each syllable, and to memorize this final teaching for the sake of passing it on to the Sangha. And yet, as I waited, no words came forth from my teacher's mouth. He sat there in silence, utterly motionless, eyes closed, conveying a sense of deep and impenetrable calm and peace such that I had never before witnessed in my many years as his servant. Clearly, the Buddha's consciousness was receding, the Blessed One was leaving this world and embarking on the final step into nirvana. And yet, with what must have been an enormous summoning of strength which willed his body to continue to function for yet a few more moments, he slowly opened his eyes and spoke...for the final time.

"Oh Ananda, how wonderful, how sublime, how beautiful. Oh Ananda, the Self that is there for all to see, in the smile of a child, in the eyes of a loved one, in the voice of a friend. The aggregates will fall away, the body will decay, the transient something that is the superficial self will indeed disappear, but the true Self that is glimpsed behind the transient self – that will always be.

"How so? Alas, Ananda, that I cannot explain. No, I cannot express through the medium of words, which are a product of our limited capacity to understand the world using the limiting means of our body and its senses, that which is of another nature altogether. How can one express that which is truly independent of the limiting realm of time and space and embodiment and all of the limiting, constricting aspects of this human life? No. Ananda, I will say no more about the Self, for by doing so I will risk committing another error.

"The Self...that which was my dear mother, that which was my beloved wife, that which was my precious son, that which was my brave father, that which was my countless devoted disciples, that which is you, and that which is me. Yes, Ananda, it truly is, and always has been, and always shall be. The mystery of the Self...in the mysterious realm where words have died. The mystery of the Self which is manifested but darkly through the limitations of our senses in the limiting conditions of our body in the limited realm of space and time. The mysterious Self, in its manifold forms, immersed in time and space as you and me and others, yet sublimely transcendent and touched not by space and time and duality. The mystery of the Self. See it, Ananda, embrace it, cherish it. The true Self. The Self that is our original face, before there was time, space, form and being. The pure, clear, loving, Self. What bliss!"

Chapter 8

Ananda's Closing

I sat in utter stillness, waiting for the next word to come from the mouth of the Blessed One. But no word came. Surely he would elucidate further on this new teaching about the nature of the self, which was both radically different from the dharma that he had previously taught and – at least to my limited mind – still quite puzzling. The Buddha had taught for years in a style that was precise, clear, and logical. But these remarks which I had just heard about the self – was it dharma, was it poetry, was it (I feel ashamed to even suggest such a thing) the confused product of the Buddha's diminished mind as it headed toward death? This new teaching was full of mystery, full of puzzles and paradoxes, full of what seemed to be more like a poetic attempt to express the inexpressible than a precise declaration of reality as it is.

Yes, I waited and waited. I waited as I had done many times before, knowing that the Blessed One delivered the dharma according to his own inclination. And yet, as I waited longer and longer, still no words came.

He sat there, eyes closed, in perfect lotus position, with spine erect and that soft half-smile with which I had become so familiar as a sign of deep contentment. No words came from his mouth, and yet in a sense that I truly cannot describe, I had a vague sense that he was nonetheless transmitting something to me, transmitting a wordless dharma which I was slowly absorbing without entirely comprehending. It was as if he was making a deposit of dharma in my mind in order that it might be available for future generations of followers of the Buddha's path. I sat silently, the Buddha sat silently – for well over two hours, into the hour approaching dawn.

I was utterly transfixed by the calm, still, peaceful figure of the Buddha, radiating a sense of such profound equanimity as to seemingly calm the very air in the room and quiet the sounds of the night outside the window. Such an extraordinary moment of profound peacefulness.

Suddenly, I became aware of a change in the room – something subtle, but nevertheless very distinct, even powerful, and ever so slowly increasing in intensity. I sensed that the room was getting warmer, as if heat was radiating from the still body of the Buddha. A sweet fragrance filled the room – oh, such a delicious sweetness as I had never before experienced, filling the air and saturating each in-breath which transported the heavenly sweetness deep inside me and transformed my inner body into an abode of indescribable bliss.

A vibration filled the air, at first barely perceptible, but then gradually increasing to an intensity that seemed to threaten to shatter the entire room if not for the exquisite harmony of the vibration – a vibration that penetrated my body and every cell in my body and was in complete synchronicity with the divine fragrance that likewise had entered me. Indeed, the fragrance, the warmth, the vibration – perhaps it was just one single experience, perhaps it was multiple experiences of the infinite ineffable modes of sheer bliss. Whatever it was that was happening to me, it was as if I had entered into a completely new mode of being and had acquired capacities of sensation far more subtle and profound than anything that I had ever before experienced in my many decades of traveling through this world in a human form.

And then the light, such as I never before seen – throughout the room, the light acquired a shimmering, luminescent, ethereal quality. Such color! Or perhaps it was no color, just clear light. Or perhaps it was both. Again, words to describe it simply escape me. I can only say that it was a pure, pristine, immaculate light which bathed the entire room, including my body.

And still there was more! From the still body of the seated Buddha there came forth brilliant rays of golden light of such intensity that I felt utterly overwhelmed, craving to close my eyes in the presence of such sacred light, yet so utterly incapacitated by all that was flooding my senses that I could not even perform the simple act of shutting an eyelid. The light seemed to penetrate the pores of my skin, filling my body and transforming me into a vessel of pure light. I sat there, transfixed, unable to move, unable to speak, yet bathed in such a profound state of contentment that I could have remained there forever.

What was happening to me? Was I still 'me'? Was I Ananda? Was I the Buddha? Was I both?

And then, just as abruptly as it had begun, this sublime experience of divine sensations ceased, and I found myself again sitting there in front of the still form of the Blessed One. Everything about the room had returned to normal. It was simply the Blessed One and me, sitting across from each other, the Buddha still seated as if in meditation, myself seated but hardly meditating, as my mind attempted to recover from not only the extraordinary experience that had just overwhelmed my senses, but also, and perhaps of an even more extraordinary nature, the words of the Buddha that I had been listening to this evening.

I looked at the Buddha. His features had resumed a normal appearance. He was simply sitting there, in the lotus position, eyes closed, exuding the sense of calmness that I had observed countless times during my many years with him. Indeed, so familiar was his posture and countenance that for a moment I wondered if the bewildering events of the evening had not really happened. Perhaps it all had been nothing more than a dream, or an illusion brought about by a fever or poor digestion. And yet, I knew that such was not the case. Although I had not yet achieved the blessed state of enlightenment,[49] I had progressed far enough in my development of mindfulness and insight that I could clearly distinguish between what was real and what was illusory, and the events of this night, however much I wished they had been the product of my imagination, had indeed been real.

Many moments passed, as we quietly sat there, the Buddha deep in samadhi, myself incapacitated by exhaustion. And then, much to my delight and surprise, the Blessed One slowly opened his eyes. Gazing directly into my eyes, with that penetration that I had come to both treasure and dread, he remained silent while the slightest smile slowly appeared on his face. What a wonderful moment this was for me, and one which I will always treasure – the Blessed One, the bringer of dharma, silently blessing me with his soft gaze and smile. After only a few moments of this, his body began to move. It was such a smooth, controlled, sublime, even beautiful sort of movement that I was somewhat entranced by it as he slowly shifted out of the lotus position and stretched out on his right side, left arm extended on top of his left leg, right arm folded as a pillow to rest his head. The Buddha had assumed the position of the Lion's Roar, the ideal position in which to prepare for death. His eyes were closed as he descended into the reclining position, but once fully reclined in the Lion's Roar, he briefly opened his eyes one last time, and spoke: "Goodbye Ananda. May you be happy and well. Remember what you have heard this night, and share it fully with the Sangha. Goodbye my friend."

And with that, he breathed his last breath. The Buddha was dead.

There are important events in a man's life which demand a full accounting, one containing a profusion of wisely chosen words to recount in the most minute detail both the enormity of the event and the nature of its impact on the writer. But there are other events that are of such a profound, shattering, ineffable nature that few words are needed, since all the words in the world would still be utterly inadequate. Such is the case in describing my reaction to the death of the Buddha. There is no point in attempting to describe the thoughts and feelings that exploded inside my heart and mind when the Blessed One left this world in my presence. So I will say no more about that moment and its immediate aftermath. The details of the aftermath of the Buddha's death, including his cremation and the subsequent distribution of his relics, can be found elsewhere.[50] I will humbly end my contribution to this account of the Blessed One's final teaching during his final night, by addressing my current status and the status of this sutra, as I complete its writing, sitting here in my hut, five years after that wonderful and dreadful night.

Epilogue

The above account of the last night of the Buddha was written by me on the day after the Buddha's death. I am renowned for my capacity to memorize everything that I hear, and I am credited with flawlessly memorizing the 82,000 teachings of the Buddha which were later recorded in writing to provide a lasting record of the Blessed One's teachings. But the extraordinary nature of what was taught by the Buddha on his final night was such that I could not risk forgetting even a single syllable. Indeed, I feared that because of the deeply troubling implications of what he had taught and the profound consequences that it was likely to mean for me and the entire Sangha, my normally infallible mind might wish to erase or alter the shattering words of the evening, and hence to avert such an error I diligently wrote them down the very next day. But all did not proceed as expected.

As I write this final note, it is forty years since the Buddha's parinirvana, I have reached the ripe age of 120 years, and after years of slow decline, I can sense that the vital breath shall soon leave my body and I too will find death and whatever follows. But before my last breath, I wish to record for posterity what has occurred during the many years since I received the Buddha's deathbed confession.

On that night, the Blessed One gave me an order: he explicitly instructed me to share this correction to his teaching with the entire Sangha. As with any command from my Teacher, I initially intended to obey it completely. Disobedience was unimaginable. And yet, as I weighed the shocking nature of this teaching, the reaction of my fellow monks, and the potential consequences that I would have to deal with, I found myself, for the first time in my life, frozen with fear. I was terrified by the thought that my brothers would not believe me. Why should they believe me? I had no witness! Why should anyone believe that, in the waning moments of his life, this perfect enlightened being would acknowledge that he had taught in error? How absurd! Indeed, if another monk had approached me with such a story, I would have dismissed him as either mad or under the spell of the evil one, Mara. Surely, I would receive similar treatment: I would be reviled, scorned, humiliated, cast out of the Sangha.

In this troubled state of mind I delayed communicating the Buddha's teaching from that night to anyone. For weeks I was racked with worry and despair, moment to moment changing my mind about what to do, and then changing it back again. It was while I was in this state of despair that, shortly after the Blessed One's death, the venerable Mahakashyapa[51] informed me that a council would be convened of all arhats[52] in the city of Rajagriha, in order to preserve the complete, definitive collection of the Buddha's teachings. And I, as the guardian of the dharma, would play the key role of reciting all of the Buddha's teachings to my fellow monks.

It was at this moment that I should have revealed to Mahakashyapa the true nature of that last night with the Blessed One. But I remained silent.

And when the council convened, I dutifully recited, word for word, syllable by syllable, all of the Buddha's teachings. All except one.

Of that final night with the Buddha, I recited only those words which were uttered up until the beginning of what has been communicated in this present document. What I recited regarding that final night contained the Buddha's teaching only up to that chilling moment when he first awoke from a slumber and declared that he had taught in error. And what I recited at Rajagriha, along with the account of the days leading up to that final night, is what has become known as the *Mahaparinirvana Sutra*. And I, Ananda, do now declare, in great shame and regret, that the *Mahaparinirvana Sutra* is an incomplete account of that final night. A full account of that fateful night, and a full account of the last teaching of the Buddha, must also include the teachings included here, teachings that I know will be rejected as false by the entire Buddhist community, teachings that will lead to my banishment from the Sangha and shame forever associated with my name.

But I must obey the Blessed One. It is an act of obedience that has been delayed by forty years of cowardice and fear, but it is an act that must be done.

It is done.

Chapter 9

Some Concluding Remarks

And so ends the *Deathbed Sutra of the Buddha*, leaving behind a multitude of questions about its content, its authenticity, its history and much more. Before closing, let us briefly examine some of these issues that are likely to ignite intense debate in the Buddhist community, among both scholars and practitioners.

To begin, there is the mystery of what happened to the *DBS* from the time of its composition in the 5th century BCE to its rediscovery in the 21st century. Ananda's concluding remarks are somewhat puzzling: he states that he did not inform Mahakashyapa of the *DBS* or recite it at Rajagriha, but he also declares that he has obeyed the Buddha's command to communicate his final teaching to the Sangha. How do we explain this apparent contradiction?

In light of the lack of additional evidence, we can only speculate: perhaps, despite his intentions to obey the Buddha, Ananda succumbed to the fear of what would happen to him if he presented such a potentially inflammatory work to the leaders of the early Sangha. Ananda's reputation has remained untarnished in Buddhist legend: would this be the case if he had revealed and become identified with the *DBS*?

Perhaps, intending to share the *DBS* with others within the community only as he approached the end of his life in order to avoid having to endure years of ostracism, he died suddenly without having the opportunity to pass on the text to his fellow monks. Or perhaps, shortly before his death, he did share the *DBS* with the leadership of the early Sangha, who found its content to be so objectionable that they suppressed its dissemination. All of these scenarios are possibilities, and yet the true story will perhaps remain forever unknown. The initial disappearance of the *DBS* is as much, if not more, of a mystery as its recent reappearance.

The question of the authenticity of the *DBS* will be challenged by many, and for good reason, in light of the curious circumstances of its recent appearance after such a long absence and its doctrinal conflict with traditional Buddhist dharma, including that which is found in the other Pali sutras. Nonetheless, I would like to suggest that regardless of the origin and authenticity of the document, the *DBS* raises some significant issues and challenges for our understanding of the Buddhist dharma. Indeed, even if the *DBS* is not an authentic sutra taught by the Buddha, and even if the *DBS* was just composed yesterday, its content deserves serious consideration, in that it articulates, through the supposed words of the Buddha (and whether they are or are not the words of the Buddha is quite irrelevant), ideas that challenge the traditional Buddhist understanding of the self, the world, and the nature of spiritual enlightenment. The vehicle (the *DBS*) may be flawed, but the contents which it delivers are nevertheless valuable and worthy of serious examination. Our remaining remarks will briefly reflect on the content of the *DBS*, leaving the issue of the historical authenticity of the work for others to pursue.

A word of caution is in order, however, before we proceed to examine the content of the *DBS* in comparison to what 'Buddhism says.' No religion is monolithic. Within Christianity we have not only the differences between the Roman Catholic, Protestant, and Orthodox branches, but also the countless variations within Protestantism, from fundamentalist to mainstream to liberal interpretations of the nature and content of Christian faith. In Islam, we have the differences between Sunni and Shi'a; in Judaism, differences between Orthodox, Conservative, and Reform interpretations; in Hinduism, a bewildering diversity of positions, some based on allegiance to different conceptions of the deity (Vaishnava, Shaivite, etc.), some based on theological positions (Advaita Vedanta, Sankhya, etc), yet others based on styles of spirituality (the karma, bhakti, and jnana *margas*). Buddhism likewise displays such a rich diversity, with the root distinction between Hinayana (which itself is said to have had fourteen different schools) and Mahayana, the uniqueness of Vajrayana (with four distinct branches in the Tibetan tradition), and the multiple schools within Mahayana that range from strict monasticism to popular lay Buddhism. Hence, to the extent that we make reference to 'Buddhist' beliefs, it is necessarily in the context of recognizing that over the centuries, Buddhism has developed into a multi-faceted tradition with a wide range of theological, philosophical, and spiritual positions.

Our concern here, in fact, is not so much with any generically 'Buddhist' assertions, as it is with the position expressed in a very specific set of Buddhist texts, namely the Pali Sutras. Buddhism, of course, has a multiplicity of sacred texts, and the Pali Sutras exist only in the context of this much larger universe of sutras, many radically different in nature from the Pali works. Nonetheless, it is fair to say that every religious tradition, however diverse its body of sacred texts might be, has a *foundational* text or set of texts that are identified as originating closer to the origins of the tradition and consequently carring a weight of authority that gives them a privileged position within that multiplicity of sacred writings. In the case of Buddhism, the foundational texts (in the eyes of practitioners as well as scholars) are, of course, the Pali Sutras, which are recognized (again, by both practitioners and scholars) as the closest thing we have to the actual words of the Buddha. Editing, redacting, and various revisionist re-workings may very well have occurred prior to the creation of the Pali texts in their current form, but they nonetheless are generally recognized as the earliest collection of the Buddha's teachings, and as such they serve as foundational texts for all three branches of Buddhism: Hinayana, Mahayana, and Vajrayana. Consequently, what is said in the Pali texts represents authoritative Buddhist teaching, accepted by all of the diverse schools that grew out of these early texts. Hence, their importance to Buddhism is immeasurable: what is said by the Buddha in the Pali texts is *important*. And consequently, by virtue of the fact that the *DBS* challenges what is said in the traditional rendering of the Pali texts, the *DBS* has significance for the entire Buddhist tradition.

The Pali Sutras profess to be the actual words of the Buddha. Most of the sutras begin with the standard phrase, "Thus have I heard..." followed by a description of the location of the sutra, the audience for the sutra, the circumstances surrounding the teaching, and, lastly and most importantly, the actual words of the Buddha, often conveyed in dialogue with a Buddhist monk, a lay follower, an antagonist, and others. In light of the nature of the Pali texts as the words of the Buddha, perhaps a more fruitful approach to examining the significance of the content of the *DBS* is to consider it as an expression of *what the Buddha said and taught*, in contrast to the Pali text account of *what the Buddha said and taught*, rather than comparing the *DBS* to the broader, generic, and inevitably misleading notion of what 'Buddhists' teach, believe, etc.

In broad terms, then, how does what the Buddha taught in the *DBS* differ from what the Buddha taught in the previously-known Pali Sutras? What is the essential uniqueness of what the Buddha teaches in the *DBS*? Distilling the many words that are attributed to the Buddha in this purported final conversation with Ananda, what is the heart of this teaching, and how does it represent a departure from the positions presented by the Buddha elsewhere in the Pali canon?

In specific terms, the teachings of the Buddha in the *DBS* depart from the broader Pali Sutra teachings in two ways. First, in the *DBS* the Buddha presents a radically different understanding of the nature of the self. This contrast is presented quite clearly in chapter seven of the *DBS*. Here the Buddha modifies (or, some might say, completely rejects), the teaching on the nature of the self as found in the rest of the Pali Sutras and, indeed, is considered a fundamental tenet of Buddhism in general. In contrast to his teaching in the other sutras where the Buddha asserts that the self is nothing more than a temporary collection of aggregates (*skandhas*) with no essential nature, in the *DBS* he speaks of an elusive but nonetheless real nature of the self, which is something that should be appreciated as precious and wonderful. Secondly, while in the traditional Pali Sutras sensory perception is seen as an impediment to spiritual enlightenment and the data derived from sensory experience are viewed as obstacles,[53] in the *DBS* the Buddha clearly embraces a specific mode of perception of the world. Granted, in the *DBS* the Buddha acknowledges that sensory perception presents many pitfalls to the spiritual seeker (as in for example, the identification of what is transient as permanent, or the constant grasping for sensory experience), but he also asserts that a very specific type of sensory experience has (to use contemporary terms) spiritual value, and can indeed lead to enlightenment. Whereas in the traditional sutras the Buddha cautions against the dangers of all sensory experience, in the *DBS* he expresses regret over such a teaching and laments that he has failed to communicate to his followers the wonderful nature of certain specific ways of experiencing the world.

Hence, in his description of the true nature of the self and in his valuation of at least certain types of sensory experience, the Buddha's *DBS* teachings depart radically from the teachings that were initially presented in the traditional collection of Pali Sutras and subsequently became standard dogma (to the extent that Buddhist positions can be referred to as such) in all Buddhist schools. However, the significance of this contrast between the *DBS* and other Pali teachings is far more profound than a mere doctrinal dispute. Rather, they point to a much more profound difference: The *DBS* and the traditional Pali Sutras present two radically different spiritualities.[54] The path to spiritual enlightenment as found in the traditional sutras is simply not the same path as that found in the *DBS*. Or, perhaps more accurately, the *DBS* takes the spirituality of the Pali Sutras and, by dramatically altering if not outright rejecting certain key components of that spirituality, offers a spiritual path that, at least in certain respects, bears little resemblance to the Buddhist spirituality that is fairly consistently expressed in the traditional words of the Buddha. How, then do those spiritualities differ?

The spirituality of the Pali Sutras is essentially an inward-directed spirituality, in which the path to spiritual achievement (in this case, termed Enlightenment) is one which shuts out sensory perception of the external world and concentrates on the isolated inner space of pure subjectivity. It is within this open space of internal consciousness that the goal of spiritual practice is realized. Directing the consciousness to that which is perceived as outside the consciousness is taught as being an impediment to making progress on the spiritual path. This is illustrated in the very first sutra of the *Digha Nikaya*, where the Buddha describes sixty-two false views, attributing each of these errors to a misguided attachment to sensory experience of any type.

While categorizing religious experience is fraught with the dangers of over-generalization, it seems reasonable to suggest that the spirituality of the Pali canon is similar to what R.C. Zaehner calls 'soul mysticism'[55] and what F.C. Happold refers to as the 'mysticism of Isolation.'[56] In both cases, the spiritual experience that is sought by the practitioner is one which focuses inward to the exclusion of input from the outer world. This is, of course, a legitimate type of spirituality but, as we shall argue below, it is a very different spirituality from that presented in the *DBS*.

Given that the spirituality of the Pali canon excludes external phenomena as meaningful elements of the spiritual path, by extension it follows that the Pali Sutras' spirituality also exclude other persons as meaningful aspects of the spiritual path. Pali spirituality asserts the superiority of the homeless or monastic life, and as such devalues human interaction in its many forms as a component of the spiritual path. While this devaluation of human interaction as a component of spiritual practice is a constant theme throughout the sutras, it is illustrated most strikingly (and, perhaps, disturbingly) in the Buddha's Great Departure. At age 29, the Buddha quietly sneaks out of the palace during the night, leaving behind his wife, son, friends, family, etc. His action is presented as a testament to his profound desire to find the truth and achieve enlightenment, free from all suffering. From the Buddha's perspective, this may indeed be the case, but how does this event appear from a broader perspective in which all of the affected parties are considered? How does it appear in the full context of the realities within which his life was embedded at the moment of that departure? From the perspective of his wife and son, for instance, does this not appear as somewhat of a spiritually self-centered act, in which the commitments to others, the feelings of others, the needs of others, etc., are rather callously ignored? Is this not, in a sense, an act of abandonment? The *Buddhacarita* describes the touching scene outside the palace grounds where the Buddha bids his beloved horse, Kanthaka, to leave him and go back inside the palace gates.[57] To the contemporary reader, and especially to the contemporary spiritual practitioner who has acquired a sense of the sacred nature of all being, such an action, regardless of the Buddha's motivation, seems to display a touch of heartlessness.

Robert Forman pulls no punches in assessing this seeming lack of human-heartedness in the departure of the Buddha:

> Gautama Buddha faced the challenge of freeing himself and escaping the clutches of the demon, Mara, with inspiring courage. But let's face it, he summarily left Yashodhara, his wife, and Rahula, his son, thereby committing history's first recorded spousal abandonment. Never again would he face the spiritual challenge that is intimacy. What would he have done – no really, what would he have done – if Yashodhara, or any Mrs. Buddha, asked him, "Where do you really hurt inside, Gautama dear?"
>
> Honestly, I can't imagine what he would say. In all the Pali Buddhist literature, I don't know a single passage that describes how, after his night of enlightenment, he had an honest-to-goodness moment of doubt or even a regular old human emotion.[58]

Of course, the Buddha taught at length about the importance of such moral virtues as universal kindness and compassion toward all living beings, and in later Buddhism (which, admittedly, is not our primary concern here), we see the figure of the bodhisattva rise to prominence, a being who vows to forgo his or her own final nirvana until all sentient beings are likewise liberated. Such concern for others in a broad, universal sense does indeed represent a beautiful element of Buddhist ethics. And yet, it does not translate into any sense of the precious, sacred nature of any *individual* sentient being. Universal love is propounded alongside a rejection of the sacred value of the individual. Again, Forman wonders how the Buddha would have responded to such a challenge: "And what would he say if she asked, as Yashodhara very well might have, "You love all people, Gautama dear. Do you love *me* in any special way?"[59]

These aspects of the spirituality taught by the Buddha in the traditional Pali Sutras are not insignificant matters. Indeed, one might ask if the path advocated by the Buddha in the traditional Pali Sutras is, in a certain sense, spiritually problematic. Is it not in some sense, a limiting and restricted spirituality, one that teaches a path to internal quiescence (in itself, certainly a desirable achievement) but only at the expense of failing to remain open to the experience of the sacred through sensory experience, whether that be through other selves or natural phenomena?

This perceptive on the spirituality of the traditional Pali Sutras makes the content of the *DBS* all the more surprising. The *DBS* isn't just a modification of certain doctrinal teachings that the Buddha decided to refine at the last moment; the *DBS* represents a way of pursuing the spiritual path – a spirituality – that is radically different from that found in the other Pali texts. The spirituality of the traditional Pali Sutras is one that can be described as individualist (focusing on liberation acquired through leading a monastic life, with limited contact and interactions with the complex and often messy world of everyday social life) and isolationist (proposing a path to liberation that directs one's attention away from the external world and into the realm of the mind). By contrast, in the *DBS* the Buddha advocates a spirituality which can be said to include both a humanistic and naturalistic element.

The humanistic spirituality of the *DBS* can be seen in the Buddha's assertion that, despite the impermanent nature of the constituent parts that make up the temporal self, there is something else of a more essential nature that can be perceived in our interactions with other human beings. There is, so to speak, a Self behind the self, a spiritually meaningful something behind the impermanent, changing, superficial ego that we mistakenly identify as our true nature. Rather than rejecting the notion of an essential self, in the *DBS* the Buddha affirms that in our relationship with the other, there is something profoundly deep and meaningful that can be known, something that can be embraced rather than fled from, as we walk on the path to spiritual growth. In the examples of the mother's love for her child and the widower's love for his wife, the Buddha teaches that in love for another we can gain a glimpse of an aspect of that rare and precious, yet ultimately ineffable, transcendent reality that is the goal of the spiritual path. The precise nature of that which is perceived as the 'true Self' is admittedly left undefined, but this is entirely consistent with the entire body of the Buddhist dharma, where the Buddha declines requests to articulate the nature of that which cannot be expressed in words, but only known in the immediacy of direct experience.

The naturalistic element of the spirituality of the *DBS* is seen in the Buddha's reversal of the Pali canon's many injunctions to close off sensory stimuli from the external word. In marked contrast to his other teachings in the Pali texts, in the *DBS* the Buddha teaches that one can experience elements of the external, natural world in a manner that (as with experience of other selves) can be spiritually meaningful. In passages reminiscent of a type of nature mysticism (and, in an odd sense, sounding somewhat like a passage from Jewish philosopher Martin Buber's 20th century masterpiece, *I and Thou),*[60] the Buddha marvels at the wondrous, mysterious, sublime quality of the color of a leaf, the taste of a mango, and the feel of a breeze. This reflects an orientation to the natural world that is completely foreign to the traditional Pali texts. Rather than cutting off sensory input from the outside, natural world, the spirituality of the *DBS* advocates such sensory contact as something which, when done in the context of deep mindfulness without attachment or false clinging to permanence, can result in a perception of the spiritual nature of things. As such, the *DBS* presents sensitivity to and sympathy toward nature that seems quite foreign to anything found in the other

Pali Sutras.

Of course, we are not suggesting an interpretation of the *DBS* that negates the value of what is found in the other Pali texts. To suggest that the *DBS* presents a spirituality that differs from the spirituality found in the rest of the Pali canon is not to invalidate or even criticize the spirituality of the Pali Sutras. Rather, it is to suggest that the spiritual path is much broader than the somewhat restrictive path found in the Pali texts. The path of closing the portals of the senses and entering into a deep mindful awareness of what remains once the distractions of the world of impermanent, transient, phenomenal reality are eliminated, is indeed a spiritual path found not only in the Pali texts but in other renunciatory, internally-directed spiritualities. However, the *DBS* affirms that this is not the only path: there is the path that dives deeply within, but there also is the path that penetrates deeply into that which is outside the self, outside the realm of mind and consciousness. In a sense, in the *DBS* the Buddha is suggesting that, until that final fateful night of his parinirvana, the path that he had taught was an unnecessarily restricted one.

Some may acknowledge that the spirituality found in the *DBS* does indeed differ from that found in the other Pali texts, but argue that the difference is somewhat irrelevant since as Buddhism evolved, those humanistic and naturalistic elements that are lacking in the Pali Sutras eventually developed in later expressions of the Buddhist tradition. One might argue, for instance, that there is a humanistic element that shows a greater appreciation of the individual self in the Mahayana tradition with its innumerable celestial Buddhas and Bodhisattvas who are intimately concerned about the welfare of their devotees and offer a heavenly refuge into which they can be reborn as the last stage in their path to liberation from rebirth in samsara. Some might also suggest that the incorporation of tantric elements in the Tibetan Buddhist tradition, with the pairing of Buddhas and their consorts and the use of sexuality (symbolic or otherwise) as part of spiritual practice reflects a humanistic element. In addition, the influence of Confucianism exercised a humanistic influence on Buddhism as it spread into China and Japan, leading eventually to the diminished importance of celibacy and the elevation of the status of lay practitioners.

The sense of the sacred quality of the natural world also emerged in a variety of expressions of post-Pali Sutra Buddhism. Chinese and Japanese Buddhism, influenced respectively by Daoism and Shinto, present a generally appreciative attitude toward nature, and often recognize aspects of the natural word as a gateway to enlightenment. Rather than solely looking inward, these non-Indian Buddhist traditions clearly assert that opening one's awareness to a full perception of the natural realm can be a spiritually liberating experience. D.T. Suzuki offers a charming account of a conversation which reflects this sensitivity to the spiritual quality of nature:

> When a Confucian scholar visited a Zen master, he asked: "What is the ultimate secret of Zen?" The master answered: "You have a fine saying in your *Analects*: 'I have nothing to hide from you.' So has Zen nothing hidden from you."
>
> "I cannot understand," said the scholar.
>
> Later, they had a walk together along the mountain path. The wild laurel happened to be blooming. The master said: "Do you smell the fragrance of the flowering tree?" The scholar responded: "Yes, I do." "Then," declared the master, "I have hidden nothing from you."[61]

Nonetheless, while it is true that later, post-Pali Buddhism did indeed develop elements of a humanistic and naturalistic spirituality, these elements are clearly not present in the Pali Sutras. What makes the *DBS* such a remarkable document is that in this short text the Buddha teaches those very elements that are indeed absent in his other teachings in the Pali canon. While it is true that this broader understanding of the religious path, incorporating an appreciation of both the human and natural realms, is a part of later Buddhism, it certainly is not present in the traditional texts that have been preserved as the original teachings of the Buddha.

In the Pali Sutras, the Buddha characterizes his position as the 'Middle Way' between the poles of extreme asceticism and sensual indulgence. But given the extent to which the teachings in the Pali text reject the spiritual value of any sensory experience, one might argue that the Buddha's Middle Way is really not in the middle at all, but rather is a slightly less austere version of the world-rejecting asceticism practiced by the sannyasins of his day. The Buddha clearly taught the superiority of the monastic and homeless life, and as such taught in the same tradition as the broader renouncer tradition that was prevalent in northern India. Was he so immersed in the Brahmanical culture with its ascetic sannyasin ideal that he could not detach himself from a spiritual perspective that viewed contact with the world as defiling and harmful?

So in light of these various considerations (and many others that could be added), exactly what are we to make of the *Deathbed Sutra of the Buddha*? As a document, is it a rare, almost miraculous discovery, a text that is over 2,000 years old, a work that somehow survived despite being unknown to the world for two millennia? Is it actually the lost teaching of one of the most influential figures in the history of religions – indeed, in the history of humankind? Or is it, quite simply, a fraud or hoax? Perhaps a document created using the many tools of modern word processing and imaging to give the appearance of great age? Perhaps the creation of a modern writer who wished to perpetuate a hoax on a sometimes gullible publishing industry and its readers? Perhaps the product of a serious-minded thinker who wished to bring to light certain aspects of Buddhism that he or she felt were not receiving sufficient attention, using the ruse of a 'lost sutra' as a tactic for getting the attention of the scholarly and Buddhist community (like the Buddha, using *upaya*, or skillful means, so to speak)? Or perhaps its origin lies somewhere in between a legitimate document from the Buddha's era and a contemporary example of literary deception. Perhaps the *DBS* was indeed written by a Buddhist at some point during the long evolution of the tradition, by someone who wished to take the humanistic and naturalistic elements that developed in certain parts of the Buddhist world and give those elements greater status by passing them off as the actual words of the tradition's founder: the *DBS* as a Buddhist document and an old document, but not a document reflecting words that were actually uttered by Siddhartha Gautama in the 6th century BCE.

In response to such speculation on the origin of the *DBS*, we only profess, at least for now, ignorance. Perhaps at some point evidence will come forth from Buddhist scholars, philologists, and others who specialize in such matters that will definitively prove the true origin of the text. In the meantime, we must simply acknowledge: we really don't know what it is.

And yet, not knowing its origin, not knowing when it was written, not knowing the true intent of its author – in a sense, none of this really matters when evaluating the work from a *spiritual* perspective. To the extent that there is anything of value in the *DBS*, it is in its content. It is in the teaching presented through the words of the Buddha, regardless of whether those words truly came from the mouth of Siddhartha or were fictionally placed in his mouth by a subsequent author.

And what is the essence of that teaching? Quite simply, it is the teaching of a spiritual path that affirms the value of both the human and the natural world. It is a teaching that affirms the value of being, in all of its infinite marvelous forms. Not just the infinitely spacious and quiescent being that we find by diving

deeply within (as is taught in the spirituality of the traditional
Pali texts), but the infinitely multiform, constantly changing,
mysteriously complex, deep and rich being of that which
confronts our consciousness in the 'world out there,' in the world
of otherness. In the Pali texts the Buddha teaches the path to
enlightenment by *diving within*; in the *Deathbed Sutra*, the Buddha
amends this teaching to include a path to enlightenment by
embracing that which is without. In the spirituality of the Pali
canon, whatever that is which is the object of the spiritual quest
– that which is variously labeled by various Buddhist schools
with words such as Emptiness, Suchness, Rigpa, and others – it
can only be accessed by directing the consciousness inward. It
cannot be accessed by directing the consciousness outward to
any aspect of the non-subjective world, whether that be the
human or non-human/natural aspects of the external word. But
in the *DBS*, the spiritual path is opened up to the world outside
the individual consciousness, to include the entire panoramic
realm of humanity and nature. In the *DBS*, all things possess the
capacity to reveal the sacred.

In a somewhat odd sense, the *Deathbed Sutra* has a peculiarly
contemporary feel, for it brings to mind more recent accounts of
the spiritual path which likewise embrace the universe as a
repository of spirit. A comparison between the Buddha and Walt
Whitman may seem rather unlikely, and yet in affirming the
precious nature of all selves and in describing the sacred quality
of a leaf or fruit, the Buddha seems to be articulating the same
'worldly mysticism' that we find in countless passages of *Leaves
of Grass*:

Swiftly arose and spread around me the peace and knowledge
　　That pass all the argument of the earth,
And I know that the hand of God is the promise of my own,
And I know that the spirit of God is the brother of my own,
And that all the men ever born are also my brothers,

And the women my sisters and lovers,
And that a keelson of the creation is love,
And limitless are leaves stiff or drooping in the fields,
And brown ants in the little wells beneath them,
And mossy scabs of the worm fence, heap'd stones, elder,
      mullein and poke-weed.[62]

And in a similar vein, the words of the *Deathbed Sutra*, uttered perhaps in the 6th century BCE, seem to be echoed in the 'worldly mysticism' of one of the giants of 20th century Jewish spirituality, Martin Buber, who, in referring to both the spheres of nature and the human, writes:

In every sphere, through everything that becomes present to us, we gaze toward the train of the eternal Thou; in each we perceive a breath of it; in every Thou we address the eternal Thou, in every sphere according to its manner.[63]

So what then, finally, are we to make of the *Deathbed Sutra*? Perhaps nothing more than a reminder that there are many approaches to the spiritual path, many ways to reach a sense of that elusive and ineffable something that adherents of each religion encounter in their own unique way, but always modified by the unique history, environment, culture, and countless other circumstances that influence, direct, and, inevitably, limit their access to Spirit. The path described in the Pali texts is a legitimate one, but it is only one among many. The *DBS* reminds us that, as has been articulated more recently by the likes of Whitman, Buber, and countless others, Spirit can be found by reaching out to embrace the world as well as by diving deeply within into the realm of consciousness that excludes the world. The spirituality of the Pali Sutras is a path to this elusive Something, but it is one path among many, and, indeed, if the *Deathbed Sutra* is genuine, not the only path within the Buddhist tradition. At a time when openness to inclusivity among spiritualities appears to be increasing and the exclusivist perspective that salvation is found in only one religion is (with notable and significant exceptions) declining, the *Deathbed Sutra* serves as a refreshing reminder that Spirit is found through many and varied paths – even those lost for over 2000 years.

Notes

1. With reference to the title of this work, it should be noted that the original Pali document contained no title; the title was chosen by this author to reflect the nature of the text. For the sake of brevity, it will frequently be abbreviated as *DBS*. The true content of the text containing the conversation between the Buddha and Ananda, and hence, in a sense, the true 'sutra,' is found in chapters three through eight, with chapters one, two, and nine being the product of this author.

2. In Tibetan Buddhism, a *'terma'* or 'treasure' text is an ancient text that was hidden at the time of its composition by a lama or highly accomplished teacher, with the foreknowledge that it would be discovered at a later date, only when followers of the Buddhist dharma were ready to receive its teaching. Tibetan Buddhism records many accounts of the discovery of such hidden texts.

3. 'Hinayana' will be used here to refer to the earliest branch of Buddhism, with no intent of disparagement over its designation as the 'Lesser Vehicle,' in contrast to the 'Greater Vehicle' of Mahayana. We use Hinayana as an objective term to refer to the earliest branch of Buddhism, rooted in the texts of the Pali canon.

4. In 1900, a treasury of previously hidden ancient texts was

discovered by a Daoist monk in the Mogao Caves of Dunhuang, China. The hundreds of scrolls include texts on Daoism, Nestorian Christianity, and Manichaeism, but the majority of the texts are Buddhist. The contents have been distributed, sold, and otherwise dispersed to many different collections, making a comprehensive account of the contents of this rare find virtually impossible. My mysterious visitor was clearly implying that the package which he had presented to me came from Dunhuang.

5. Of course, such a belated discovery of texts from the founding era of a major religion has occurred in the Biblical tradition with the discovery of the Dead Sea Scrolls between 1946 and 1956 and the Nag Hammadi Manuscripts discovered in 1945. The Nag Hammadi manuscripts in particular are somewhat analogous to the appearance of the *Sutra on the Deathbed Reflections of the Buddha*, in that these Christian texts were buried and unknown for almost 2000 years until accidentally discovered by Egyptian farmers in 1945. Their similarity in structure to the Biblical canon is remarkable, given that they contain Gospels, Epistles, and Acts comparable to those books that are found in the New Testament. The content, however, at times diverges radically from orthodox Christian theology and traditional accounts of New Testament history. Similarly, much of the *Sutra on the Deathbed Reflections of the Buddha* is written in a style highly reminiscent of the ancient Pali texts, although the content is a shocking refutation of certain key elements of Buddhist orthodoxy.

6. Given that Buddhism in the West more commonly uses Sanskrit rather than Pali terms, we will employ Sanskrit unless otherwise noted. Commonly used Sanskrit terms (e.g., karma, dharma, nirvana, sutra) will not be italicized.

7. The history of the modern search for and eventual discovery of the birthplace of the Buddha is a fascinating tale. For an

entertaining account of this event, see Charles Allen, *The Search for the Buddha: The Men Who Discovered India's Lost Religion* (New York: Carroll and Graf, 2002).

8. See David R. Loy, *A Buddhist History of the West: Studies in Lack* (Albany: SUNY Press, 2002).

9. For a contemporary, non-Buddhist interpretation of this universal human tendency to go to great lengths to construct mortality-denying mechanisms in all aspects of everyday life, see Ernest Becker, *The Denial of Death* (New York: The Free Press, 1973).

10. It should be noted that while we refer to the Three Marks of Existence and other aspects of the dharma as 'doctrines,' this reflects the use of a Western, non-Buddhist method on conceptualizing the content of the tradition that is slightly misleading. The Three Marks, for instance, are not meant to constitute propositions that one cognitively grasps or statements of faith that one assents to, but rather experienced dimensions of reality. This experiential aspect of the dharma should be kept in mind whenever we resort to the use of 'doctrine' to describe various elements of Buddhism.

11. As found, for example, in *Majjhima Nikaya*, Sutra 63.

12. The practical nature of the dharma is nicely illustrated in the Parable of the Arrow, described in *Majjhima Nikaya*, Sutra 63. Imagine, says the Buddha, a warrior who has been wounded by an arrow. A doctor approaches the warrior to remove the arrow, treat the wound, and save the man's life. But before allowing the doctor to proceed with such life-saving measures, the wounded man insists on getting answers to many questions ("Who shot me? What tribe is he from? How old is he? Is he tall or short?") and many other questions that have no relevance to providing the warrior with the care that he needs to save his life. If all of his questions would be answered before proceeding with treatment, the warrior would die.

In a similar manner, suggests the Buddha, we would die if we took the time to first answer the multitude of philosophical questions that surround spiritual topics such as the self and the afterlife. Like the wounded warrior, we are headed toward death, and it would be wise to not waste time on irrelevant discussion; rather, given the finite duration of our existence, we should focus on the practical steps that lead to enlightenment and liberation from re-birth, as found in the Four Noble Truths. There is no time for excessive, abstract speculation for beings that are destined for death.

13. A summary of the life and significance of Ananda, as well as accounts of other important early followers of the Buddha can be found in Nyanaponika Thera and Hellmuth Hecker, *Great Disciples of the Buddha: Their Lives, Their Works, Their Legacy* (Boston: Wisdom Publications, 2003).

14. Found in the *Digha Nikaya*, Sutra 16.

15. *Digha Nikaya*, 3.1.2

16. Shortly after the death of the Buddha, Ananda was the subject of many criticisms by his fellow monks at the first Buddhist Council at Rajagriha. For a succinct summary of these criticisms, see *Great Disciples of the Buddha*, 179-182.

17. 'Tathagata' is a term used to refer to an enlightened being, literally meaning 'thus gone,' as in one who has gone forth from the world of samsara and achieved nirvana.

18. *The Last days of the Buddha: The Maha Parinibbana Sutta*, translated by Sister Vajira and Francis Story (Kandy: Buddhist Publication Society1988), p. 32.

19. Ibid, p. 66.

20. Ananda is referring here to the Buddha's use of *upaya*, or 'skillful means.' The Buddha varied the manner in which he presented the dharma in accordance with the ability of his audience to comprehend it. Simple declarative statements, elaborate metaphors, lengthy parables, and other modes of

expression were used, sometimes to the initial confusion of his followers.

21. In the Buddhist tradition we find a belief in multiple hells. One tradition enumerates eight hot and eight cold hells. The sufferings of life in a hell realm are graphically depicted by the Buddha in Sutra 130 (Devaduta *Sutta*) of the *Majjhima Nikaya*.

22. The patience of the Buddha had been severely tested when Devadatta (like Ananda, a cousin of the Buddha) attempted to replace the Buddha as leader of the Sangha. See Bhikku Nanamoli, *The Life of the Buddha* (Seattle: Buddhist Publication Society, 1972), 257-272.

23. *Majjhima Nikaya*, p.448.

24. Taking the robe and bowl is a reference to adopting the vows of a Buddhist monk, which, among other commitments, includes the use of a begging bowl for daily alms rounds and the wearing of a modest robe.

25. A Buddhist monk.

26. The Buddha had one child, a son named Rahula (which, quite tellingly and quite relevant to the content of the teaching of the *Deathbed Sutra*, means 'fetter'). Like many of Siddhartha's family members and friends from his pre-enlightened life, Rahula became a follower of his father and eventually joined the Sangha as a monk.

27. Greed, hatred and delusion are often identified in Buddhism as the three root afflictions of the unenlightened mind.

28. Mara, as lord of the realm of desire, functions as a 'tempter' in many of the narratives of the enlightenment of the Buddha. Prior to achieving enlightenment, Siddhartha undergoes various assaults on his meditative composure by Mara, who attempts to deter the soon-to-be-Buddha from achieving enlightenment through a variety of distractions and temptations. The encounter between Mara and the Buddha bears a curious resemblance to the temptations

presented to Jesus by Satan. In each case, temptation by an evil spiritual being immediately precedes the beginning of both Jesus' and the Buddha's ministry.

29. *Majjhima Nikaya*, Sutra 63.
30. *The Buddhacarita* offers a lengthy, detailed, and rather touching account of Siddhartha's final parting with his horse, Kanthaka, and groom, Chandaka. See E.H. Johnston, *Ashvaghosha's Buddhacarita or Acts of the Buddha* (Delhi: Motilal Banarsidass, 1984), 81 – 91.
31. The Vinaya is the detailed code of rules which is followed by Buddhist monks.
32. Of the four castes which constituted the Indian social structure at the time of the Buddha, Brahmins were the highest and shudras the lowest.
33. The Buddha is making reference to the traditional four stages (*ashramas*) of life in Indian society. Following the Student stage in which one is cared for by parents and is free from independent duties, one enters into the Householder stage, which typically includes marriage, children, establishing a separate household, an occupation, accumulating wealth, and similar worldly tasks. Later in life, after one has accumulated sufficient wealth to provide for one's family, it is permissible to enter the 'Forest Dweller' stage, most worldly attachments are severed and serious pursuit of the spiritual life begins. This is followed by the final stage of the *sannyasin*, or wandering ascetic, who has renounced all worldly ties. The Buddha, of course, broke from this model by advocating the 'Middle Way' which does not require extreme asceticism.
34. The 'monkey mind' is a common phrase used in the Indian yogic/meditative traditions to describe the tendency of our mind to constantly jump from one thought to another, just like the constant activity of a monkey who tirelessly swings from one vine to the next.

35. *Shamatha,* or quiescence, is one of several words used to describe the deep quieting of the mind that occurs as the result of prolonged meditation practice and is a preliminary state to the achievement of enlightenment.

36. After hearing the Buddha teach, Ambapali, a royal courtesan renowned for her exquisite beauty and charm, renounced the worldly life, joined the Sangha, and donated her mango grove to the Buddha as a retreat during the rainy season. Several of the Pali Sutras are set in Ambapali's mango grove.

37. *The Satipatthana Sutra,* as found in the *Majjhima Nikaya,* Sutra 10.

38. Here the Buddha is referring to the frequently paired aspects of meditative experience: quiescence (*shamatha*) and insight (*vipassana*).

39. Ananda was chastised by his follow monks for a number of reasons, including his suggestion that minor rules for the Sangha could be set aside and the delay in his achievement of enlightenment.

40. During his ministry, the Buddha consistently declined to engage in any extensive metaphysical speculation on the nature of reality, but here he hints at the notion of *advaita,* or non-dualism, which was a prominent school in Hindu thought and later achieved similar status in Buddhism in concepts such as *Shunyata* (Emptiness) and *Tathata* (Suchness).

41. *Majjhima Nikaya,* Sutra 51, p. 443.

42. *Majjhima Nikaya,* Sutra 51, p. 448.

43. *Majjhima Nikaya,* Sutra 87, p. 718.

44. The Buddha admitted women to full status as monks in the Sangha, but only with reluctance. See, for instance, the *Culla Vagga,* 10.1 (in Henry Clarke Warren, *Buddhism in Translation* (New York: Atheneum Press, 1976).

45. This is illustrated, for instance, in the *Culamalunkya Sutra* (*Majjhima Nikaya,* Sutra 63, pp. 533-536.

46. A modern reader of the Pali Sutras is likely to find the repetitive use of phrases, sentences, and even entire paragraphs to be rather puzzling. But repetition was an intentional literary device necessitated by the fact that these teachings were initially transmitted orally, and hence the use of repetition served as an aid in memorization.

47. Here the Buddha's teaching bears an uncanny resemblance to what would not appear until almost 2,500 years after the Buddha's death, in the I-Thou spirituality of the twentieth century Jewish philosopher Martin Buber. See Martin Buber, *I and Thou* (New York: Charles Scribner's Sons, 1970).

48. Again, see the *Culamalunkya Sutra*.

49. According to Buddhist tradition, Ananda did not achieve enlightenment until the night before the commencement of the first Buddhist Council at Rajagriha.

50. As described in the *Mahaparinirvana Sutra* of the *Digha Nikaya*, Sutra 16.6.23-28.

51. Mahakashyapa, a companion of Ananda, is traditionally referred to as the 'father of the Sangha.' In Zen Buddhism, Mahakashyapa is revered as the disciple to whom the Buddha communicated direct, mind-to-mind transmission of the dharma, and hence, in a sense, functioned as the spiritual successor to the Buddha.

52. An enlightened monk.

53. See, for instance, the *Bramajala Sutta*, the very first sutra of the *Digha Nikaya*, in which the Buddha describes no less than 62 false views, most of which involve errors that derive from the false knowledge that is acquired from sensory perception.

54. We deliberately refer to the teachings of the Buddha, whether in the traditional Pali canon or in the *DBS*, as spiritualities rather than mere 'doctrines,' since they are taught as comprehensive paths to spiritual liberation. They are more than just cognitive speculation; they are

prescriptions for a comprehensive way of life that leads to the highest good: spiritual enlightenment.

55. Jeffrey Kripal offers an insightful account of R.C. Zaehner's categories of mystical experience in *Roads of Excess, Palaces of Wisdom: Eroticism and Reflexivity in the Study of Mysticism* (Chicago: University of Chicago Press, 2001), pp. 156-198. Or see Zaehner's own *Mysticism: Sacred and Profane* (London: Oxford University Press, 1957).

56. See F.C. Happold, *Mysticism: A Study and an Anthology* (London: Penguin Books, 1970).

57. Ashvaghosha, *The Buddhacharita or Acts of the Buddha*, translated by E.H. Johnston (Delhi: Motilal Banarsidass, 1984), pp. 88-91.

58. Robert Forman, *Enlightenment Ain't What It's Cracked Up to Be* (Alresford, UK: O Books, 2011), pp.132-133.

59. Ibid., p. 133.

60. Martin Buber, *I and Thou*, translated by Walter Kaufman (New York: Charles Scribner's Sons, 1970).

61. D.T. Suzuki, *Zen Buddhism* (New York: Doubleday Anchor, 1956), p. 251.

62. Walt Whitman, *Selections from Leaves of Grass* (New York: Avenel Books, 1966), pp. 3-4.

63. Martin Buber, *I and Thou*, p. 57.

BOOKS

O is a symbol of the world, of oneness and unity. In different cultures it also means the "eye," symbolizing knowledge and insight. We aim to publish books that are accessible, constructive and that challenge accepted opinion, both that of academia and the "moral majority."

Our books are available in all good English language bookstores worldwide. If you don't see the book on the shelves ask the bookstore to order it for you, quoting the ISBN number and title. Alternatively you can order online (all major online retail sites carry our titles) or contact the distributor in the relevant country, listed on the copyright page.

See our website www.o-books.com for a full list of over 500 titles, growing by 100 a year.

And tune in to myspiritradio.com for our book review radio show, hosted by June-Elleni Laine, where you can listen to the authors discussing their books.

MySpiritRadio